Flaggadoo's Alley

. . . Trying to shy away from the argument, Stix wandered over to the grate. He stooped over and shaded his eyes, attempting to spot the reflection of at least one quarter. He wished that he and Ella could just leave and forget about the stupid corner, but he knew they had to get the quarters back first. At least that's what he told himself, but there was another reason that made him want to stay. It had to do with Mattie. Every time he looked at the old woman he felt things churning inside, things he couldn't understand or explain. He remembered his fantasy . . . how he wanted to meet new people . . . exciting people. First, he'd be afraid, and then he'd feel confused. He even thought he felt sorry for her. But he wasn't sure about that. A few times he wanted to laugh at the way she looked and acted. But he didn't dare. Stix looked back at his sister and the old woman. They were staring at each other with the oddest expressions. Words flashed through his mind: strangers . . . junkies . . . drunks . . . dangerous! However, as he gazed at the woman, the name baglady just didn't seem to fit, yet surely she was a street person, homeless and forgotten . . .

Flaggadoo's Alley

A CHILDREN'S NOVEL

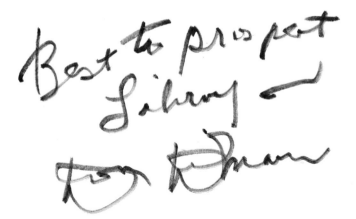

*Best to prospect
Library —
Don DiMarco*

Don DiMarco

Illustrator:

Barbara Ann Dimond

Xlibris Corporation
1-888-795-4274
www.Xlibris.com
Orders@Xlibris.com
17099

Contents

DIMOND

CHAPTER I

SAME OLD FIGGSVILLE

The lawn mower sputtered and choked before dying in a puff of blue smoke. Stix Collins pushed it toward the storage shed. The warm August breeze caught his wavy, dark hair sending it in a swirl about his head. He was taller than most kids his age, lanky and trim. For the most part Stix was fussy and neat about his appearance, except for this morning. Today, everything about him was a mess. His tanned cheeks were smudged with grease, he had a hole in the seat of his pants, and his shirt was on inside out. From the moment Stix got out of bed, he knew it was going to be a bad day. Last night's storm had kept him awake half the night. And with Ella talking in her sleep, gibbering about spiders crawling all over her, he hardly had a chance to close his eyes. Even with the bedroom door closed and two pillows stacked tightly over his head, he still heard every word his sister mumbled. Twice she screamed, bringing Stix to a sudden wide-eyed sitting position. Stix was so groggy when the alarm went off that he tripped on a sneaker while getting out of bed and fell square onto one of his favorite model cars, smashing it to smithereens. And when Aunt Jenny served oatmeal and prune juice for breakfast, he knew the day would be a total loss.

At least that's another lawn finished, he thought, pausing by the driveway where Mr. Bowman's car was parked. The bright red station wagon glimmered in the warm, morning sun. His reflection in the shiny front fender stopped him cold. He wiped his face with a sweat-covered forearm, smearing the grease downward toward his mouth. Stix laughed at his clown-like resemblance, sticking out his tongue and puffing out his cheeks. He fell back into a sitting position on the gravel driveway, resting his folded arms over his bent knees.

"I should have stayed in bed," he muttered. *But why should I?* he thought, almost as though he expected an argument from himself. *Other than mowing grass there's so much I want to do. I want to go places . . . meet people.* He closed his eyes and envisioned a million faces and a million places. How he loved each daring dream. He locked his arms over his knees and rocked back and forth, the fine gravel crunching beneath him. Images . . . wishes . . . floating by like fluffy clouds on a windy day. Stop, forward, slow motion, like VCR tapes playing to the commands of his very own remote control. "Ah!" he sighed.

Ella turned on the hose, and with a wrist-flicking, teasing motion she sprayed water near him. Just as a few sprinkles landed on Stix's head, she turned the nozzle away. Stix jerked forward shaking his head and blinking his eyes. His dreams faded into the breeze.

"Here, you're going to need it, Stix. What a mess you are," said Ella handing her brother the hose. "I'll get some soap and a towel."

Stix held the nozzle over the back of his head. The cool water felt refreshing, but the liquid soap wasn't one of his favorite brands.

"Wow, this stuff sure smells terrible."

"Gets the dirt off," Ella said, pitching her brother an old towel. "Mr. Bowman probably used this to polish his station wagon."

Stix took a whiff of the towel. "So what if I smell a little like car polish." He finished drying, then turned his shirt right side out. "You know something, Ella? I'm sick and tired of mowing lawns and pulling weeds."

"Me too!" Ella answered from inside the shed. "But remember you're the one who made that crazy deal with dad." She kicked the dew-coated grass from her sneakers. "A hundred and fifty bucks is a ton of money."

"Yeah Ella, but you want a dog, too."

"A dog . . . sure I want a dog. But a Siberian husky, huh-ah." Shaking her head briskly, Ella grumbled, "Sure wish there was another way to earn the money." She picked up the gas can and pointed to the ground. "Hand me that rake. I'll put it away."

Stix gave it a lazy pitch. Ella caught it with one hand. "Hey, not a bad catch," Stix said, as he pushed the mower into a corner of the shed, giving it a light kick. "Lately, I've begun to wonder about whether our plan to buy that dog is really worth all this work." He rubbed his thumb over a newly formed blister, pushing gently until some fluid squirted over his palm.

"Yeah, I've had it with mowing lawns, pulling weeds and raking leaves. I'm even tired of being tired. Summer is half over and we haven't really done much of anything, except mow grass."

Ella slammed the shed door and followed her brother toward the gate, her golden ponytail bouncing to the rhythm of a lively gait. "I'm bored, too. Let's go over to Jake's house. His cousin is visiting. Maybe they'll go to the park with us. I wouldn't mind playing some softball. How about it?"

Stix leaned lazily against a fence post. "No, I don't think so, Ella." He crossed his long, lean legs. What he really wanted was to get away from Figgsville, if only for a little while. He wanted to meet new people, not ordinary Figgsville folks.

"Aw, come on," Ella pleaded. "I'm getting to be a better ball player, you know. You even said it yourself."

"What do you mean?"

"Well I caught the rake with one hand, didn't I?" Her bright, green eyes flashed a glint of pride. "Couldn't have done that last year. No way!"

"That's for sure." Stix gave a half-hearted grin, nodding an unsure approval.

"That means you're going to play?"

"No!" His slight smile quickly faded, and his voice showed a tinge of irritation.

"Why not?" She wrinkled her freckled nose, a testy lower lip curled in a quiver, demanding an immediate answer.

Stix shrugged, sighing impatiently. "Being twelve can be tough, Ella."

"Why?"

"Because I have to deal with a sister who's eleven, thinks she's seventeen, and acts like she's twenty-one!"

"Twenty-one!" protested Ella. "Get off it! I never want to be that old."

"Yeah, well you sure act as if you are sometimes, and I'm not into playing ball with older people, so forget it."

Ella's eyes sagged and her lips tightened ever so slightly. It was her hurt-look face, and she knew how to turn it on and off like the TV remote control switch. Ella was an expert at getting what she wanted, more so with Stix and her friends than with her mom and dad. Aunt Jenny often called her a professional conniver.

"Come on, Stix, give me a break, I'm really not that bad of a player. I don't even strike out anymore," she swallowed hard, "well . . . not very often, when you consider the improvement I've made."

"Ella, that has nothing to do with it. I just don't want to play ball. I need a change of scenery. So forget it. Why don't you go home?"

"Come on Stix, you have it made. Why would you want a change?"

"I don't know, Ella."

Ella turned her nose up. "You don't even have a reason. Just admit it, brother. You're just trying to get rid of me."

"Why do you always argue with me?"

"Because sometimes you act so dopey. That's why."

Stix rubbed his eyes. "Dopey. I don't know about that, but if you had said tired, well then I'd have to agree with you."

Placing both hands behind his head, Stix bent backward and yawned. "Exercise! That's it. I need some exercise to help me wake up. My eyelids are drooping," he mumbled through another yawn.

"But it's almost ten thirty, and you already mowed a lawn."

He yawned again. "I can't help it. Between the storm and your weird spider nightmares, I hardly slept at all."

Ella counted the money Mr. Bowman had paid them for the lawn work. "Four dollars. Not bad for a small job."

Stix started toward the gate. "You can have it," he said indifferently without turning.

"Oh no you don't. You're not going to bribe me with a few quarters. I'm going with you. And don't pull that big brother routine. It won't work. Here, take your share." Chasing him to the sidewalk, she stuffed eight quarters into Stix's pocket. He did little to protest taking his share, but tried his best to ignore her demand to go with him.

"See you later, Ella. I have a feeling I'm going to be late getting home tonight. Might not even make it for dinner."

"I'm going too," Ella repeated louder than before.

"Oh no you're not." At first Stix raised his voice, then he settled for a mellower tone. *I can't order her around. It won't work*, he thought. *When she's angry, she's impossible.* He tried another tactic. "Aunt Jenny will be hopping mad, and if I take you along with me, well, that will mean real trouble, especially if mom and dad find out."

"Not a chance. Like I said, I'm going with you!" She tightened her jaw line, speaking firmly, "Mom and dad won't be home for at least two days. Who knows, they might even stay a little longer. They never went away without us before. A computer convention in Orlando . . . what a bummer." Stix tried to interrupt, but she wouldn't give him a whisper of a chance. "You can call Aunt Jenny and tell her we won't be home for awhile. She's good about that kind of thing, as long as she knows where we are and what we're doing." Ella walked beside her brother, each stride purposely snappy and aggressive, another way to show her stubborn determination. "Besides, I'm bored, too. Sometimes Figgsville gets to be old stuff . . . same places . . . same things . . . same people."

The stubborn streak wasn't new to Stix. He knew how tough it was to talk Ella into something she didn't want to do. And he couldn't argue about Figgsville being old stuff. Besides, Ella wasn't about to go home, no matter what he said. In a way, Stix liked the know-it-all look on his sister's face when she stuck up for herself. Stix smiled, remembering the many times Ella got into trouble because of her stubborn streak. Stix conceded. "OK smarty, you can go along. But if we get into trouble, you're on your own. Get it?" That was his way of acting tough. But he knew that Ella always held her own, like the time Punky Macko tried pushing her around at school. At first Stix was going to butt in on the fight and defend his sister. That would have been easy to do. He never much cared for the likes of Punky Macko. On second thought he remained a spectator. Good thing he did. Ella really held her own. She taught Punky a thing or two. She blasted him with verbal combat, sending the dazed bully into a tailspin of confusion and stuttering. Poor Punky! The angrier Ella got, the bigger the words she used. She stripped Punky's pride clean. Even his rowdy friends gawked in silly stupors because they didn't know what she was talking about. Eventually, Punky retreated and never messed with her again. Down deep, Stix was proud of his sister. But he wasn't about to let her know it. That's the way it was between them, always fighting each other in a quiet sort of way, except when it came to trouble. Then they stuck together like white cat hairs on stuffed black furniture.

Ella knew when to back off, too. She gave Stix a wink and wrinkled her nose. "Here we go again," she laughed. Ella's freckles seemed to dance off her face.

Stix knew what was coming. It was their special secret signal. Together they groaned, long and hard, "Boooorrrring!" It was something they did together all the time.

"Lucky mom isn't here," snickered Ella. "She can't stand it when we do that."

Now there was no doubt in Stix's mind. Ella was going with him and that was that. They crossed Main Street to a public telephone. Stix called Aunt Jenny and told her they were going for a walk.

"Where are you walking to?" he knew she'd ask.

"Nowhere special . . . just going for a walk," he answered politely, not wishing to raise her ire, or to give her cause to ask more questions. He knew how easily Aunt Jenny got rattled, and almost every time she got nervous her asthma kicked up. Stix remembered her gasping for air a couple of times. Once he swore she turned blue. "You be home for supper, and take care of Ella."

"Sure, don't worry. We'll be just fine, and believe me Aunt Jenny, Ella can take care of herself."

His sister leaned on a nearby tree with an impish smirk. She poked him in the back. "Come on! Come on! Come on!" she teased, moving from side to side as Stix slapped blindly behind his back at her jabbing fingers.

"Just the same, you keep an eye on her."

Stix pulled the phone back in a jerk as Aunt Jenny's voice grew louder. It always did when she got excited. "Is that Ella I hear in the background?" she shouted.

Ella cupped her hands, whispering, "I can hear her from here." Stix motioned for her to be quiet. Ella made a face. Stix grit his teeth, glaring at her with squinty eyes.

"She's younger than you," Aunt Jenny screeched into the phone. "And don't be getting into trouble. And another thing, don't forget . . ."

Stix rubbed his ear, now holding the phone at arm's length. "OK, Aunt Jenny . . . OK . . . OK . . . yes, I will, Aunt Jenny. Good-bye."

A jabbering mix of warnings and good-byes faded as Stix gently hung up. As the receiver clicked down, his quarter shot right out of the coin return. He caught it, flipped it in the air and smiled. "Maybe this will be my lucky day after all." Turning he said, "Come on Ella, let's get moving." But she was already halfway up the street. He raced after her shouting, "Wait for me!"

Ella waited until he was a few feet away, then stuck her freckled nose in the air, saying, "Mind what Aunt Jenny said: "I'm younger than you, so you better take care of me." She took off again laughing wildly.

CHAPTER II

THE WRONG BUS

Railroad Avenue was almost deserted, not a train in sight. Now that the Carbon Iron Works had shut down, there wasn't a need for trains. Stix loved trains, but he was lucky if he saw one a month go by. He gazed hopefully at the tracks. Only an old flat car remained set in the distance on rusting rails, still and ghost-like. It reminded Stix of old Mr. Hinton, the retired railroader, who sat stone-faced and rigid on his white wicker porch chair. When he grunted and spit tobacco, some kids made fun of him. Stix never did. To him, being different wasn't something at which to poke fun. Being different was interesting, maybe even special. He often wondered what the old man was thinking. "Maybe he's like the flat car, waiting for a powerful new engine to round the bend, hitch it up and roll away to some bustling place where old trains are still needed," he said, forgetting the presence of his sister.

"What on earth are you talking about?" asked Ella, a confused look on her face.

"Huh, oh nothing. Let's get moving." Stix took a last look at the rusting flat car and at the tracks that rounded past the dilapidated station and then faded out of sight. Like a lot of things in Figgsville lately, there was less to see and less to do. So many people seemed to be moving away. Last month two of Stix's and Ella's best friends moved because their parents were laid off from the Carbon Iron Works and couldn't find other jobs in Figgsville. Like a lot of others, they moved to the city in search of work. Stix and Ella walked aimlessly through the town, searching for something different or unusual, something new and exciting. But it wasn't easy, not in Figgsville. The street sights were so ordinary, almost as if they were part of an old painting, frozen in watercolor or dried in oil.

Across the street Mrs. O'Dell hung sheets, socks, shirts and underwear on her sagging clothesline, while her cat, Nittens, chased a mole into a flower bed.

Jeddy Parkin's stereo blared from his second floor bedroom window, his crossed legs and untied sneakers dangled from the window, swaying to the beat of the music. Two fat men with wide red suspenders snoozed in tip-backed chairs in front of the South Figgsville Fire Hall; a dazed Dalmatian lying by their sides barely lifted his head as the kids passed by. On the porch of the American Legion Hall there was a group of men playing cards. A red-faced man with a double chin was complaining as usual. He grumbled at the snapping of each card his partner played. "You threw the wrong card, Charlie. Stupid play! We could of had 'em." The others chuckled at his displeasure, except for Charlie, who never much smiled at anything.

"Nothing new," Ella whispered. "I'll bet he never wins."

Stix twisted his mouth behind the back of his hand. "Why do you think he's always complaining . . . because he's winning?" Stix jumped up on the brownstone wall that surrounded the park. He balanced with the grace of a tightrope walker. Ella staggered behind him with her arms out, trying to keep her balance. While pointing his finger at the ongoing card game, Stix muttered, "See what I mean now? It's the same old thing day after day. Don't you wish something exciting would happen around here?"

"You mean like a big fire or a robbery?"

"Naw, nothing like that."

"What do you mean, Stix? What kind of excitement are you looking for?"

"I don't know what I mean, but I'm sure sick and tired of . . ."

Officer Janosky tapped the back of a nearby park bench with his night stick. "Off the wall!" he growled. Stix stopped in a sudden jerk, and Ella, startled by the policeman's voice, turned quickly and plowed into Stix's rear.

Before jumping to the sidewalk, Stix whispered to Ella, "See what I mean. We can't even walk on a lousy stone wall without someone getting angry at us. In Figgsville you have to walk on the sidewalk because that's the way it is. A sidewalk is for walking on, and a stone wall is for keeping people out."

"Yeah," agreed Ella, "like I said, same old stuff, the *Figgsville Rut*."

"Sounds like a new soft rock dance." Stix dipped his knees and gave a few body shakes. "Do-oot-do-ah! Doo-ah, the Figgsville Rut, Do-oot-do," he sang. "Figg-a-figg-a-rut, Do-oot-do, Doo-ah!"

"What rhythm!" Ella bumped him off the curb.

They sat on a bench and laughed for awhile until Officer Janosky walked away shaking his head. Then they were on their way again, dancing and singing Figg-A-Figg-A-Doo, side by side. Stix kicked an old tin can until both ends fell off. Ella poked a stick into a nest of tent caterpillars that clung to a Maple tree limb which sagged over the edge of the sidewalk. "Ugly little critters," she said, wrinkling her nose.

Stix looked closely at the wiggling creatures. "Boy, you talk about boring. This thing has to be the pits. How would you like to live your life in a webbed tent?"

"No thanks." She gave the nest another jab.

"What are you doing that for?"

"I'm creating excitement. Even worms get bored I'll bet." Ella gave the stick one last shake. "Look at 'em go."

Stix bent over for a closer look. He took the stick from Ella's hand and poked the caterpillars as though he was stoking the last dying embers in their living room fireplace on a winter night.

"In a way this nest is just like Figgsville. Everyone doing the same old thing day in and day out." He gave one last thrust. "I doubt if an earthquake would change things around here."

They found another can and took turns kicking it. Stix yawned and moved toward the berm, letting the can sit in the middle of the road. Ella picked it up and grumbled, "Litterbug."

"Hey, come here," Stix called.

"What?" Ella looked at Stix, whose cheeks bulged with blackberries. Her eyes widened. "Oh great," she said, picking a handful exclaiming, "Gads, the bushes are loaded."

Purple juice ran down the corner of Stix's mouth. "This is more . . . chomp, chomp . . . like it . . . chomp, chomp, chomp . . . huh, Ella?"

"Can't you eat without making so much noise? You're such a sloppy eater."

He chomped louder on purpose, squishing the juice through his teeth. Then he stuck out a purple tongue. "Augggg!" Stix faked a gag.

"Go ahead," she said, daintily popping a blackberry into her mouth with a quick snap of her wrist, "You're sure to get a stomach ache. Then we'll see how silly you can act."

"What do you mean?" he protested.

Ella gave a snooty look. "You're eating so fast and snorting like a pig. It would serve you right to get sick." She closed her eyes in disgust when he squirted a few purple spit bubbles through his lips. "You're so crude sometimes," she sneered.

Ella and Stix picked and ate their way along the road, not realizing they had wandered onto Old Route 99. Neither of them had ever walked that far from home. Stix was sure his parents would be in a rage if they knew where he and Ella were. *Being grounded is the pits,* he thought. But he didn't dwell on the consequences. Ella acted more carefree. She loved the excitement of being on her own.

Cars were now whizzing by, so Stix and Ella kept to the side of the road, walking closer to the edge of the woods taking in all the sights: Rumbling trucks with tandem trailers, the kind that seldom went through Figgsville; a state police car zooming by with the siren wailing and red, white and blue lights swirling around; two road workers painting guard rail posts; a dingy diner with a faded "HOMEMADE PIES" sign swaying over the entrance and an old barn with a colorful, circular design at the top.

"Look over there . . . by the barn!" Stix pointed to an old hand water pump. They ran toward it. A sign stained with dried mud and riddled with holes read SAFE DRINKING WATER.

Stix put his finger through one of the holes and wiggled the tip of his first knuckle. "Bullet holes."

"I don't believe it." Ella picked up an old tin cup that hung by the handle. A spider crawled across her finger. She screamed and shivered.

"Come on, it's only a dumb old spider." Stix stared at his sister with a mocking twist of his head, smacking his tongue against his teeth. He folded his arms and tapped his foot. "Well, well, Miss Independent is actually afraid of something," he teased, knowing how she hated bugs, especially spiders.

"They bite." Ella winced, checking her hand carefully. She shivered again, remembering the horrible nightmare about spiders she had last night. "I hate them. I just hate them."

"What are you so afraid of?"

"Are you deaf, Stix? I said they bite! What do you need an E-Mail message? They bite. Get it?"

"Only people with sugar in their blood," Stix teased again.

Ella glared at her brother. "Stop it!" There you go trying to fool me again. When will you ever learn that I'm too smart to fall for that stupid kind of stuff?"

"I know," said Stix. "But you do eat a lot of cookies."

"Maybe so, but cookies won't kill you." She banged the cup on the cast iron water pump to be sure it was rid of spiders. "But I'll bet this water will; I'm not drinking it even if I am thirsty."

Stix started pumping the handle. Squish, squish. "I've seen pictures of these things, but I've never used one." Squish, squish. "Must be older than that antique oaken bucket." He motioned toward the right side of the pump where the moss-covered pail hung from a dead tree branch.

"Old barn, old pump, old bucket . . . this place is beginning to give me the creeps." Ella shivered. "I can't hear any water coming." Squish, squish.

Stix pumped harder. Ella put her ear to the rusted pipe. "It's gurgling. I can hear it now. Pump harder!"

"I'm pumping, I'm pumping," he gasped.

"Be quiet. I think I can hear a gurgle. Just keep pumping."

Stix puffed, "I thought you weren't going to drink the water."

"Didn't say anything about drinking it. I just want to see if it's really water I'm hearing. Could be oil, you know. Who knows, maybe we'll strike it rich."

"Get off it," ridiculed Stix.

"Ella snickered silently as she pressed her ear closer to the pipe. "It's getting louder. Pump harder!"

Perspiration dripped from Stix's forehead. He pumped harder and faster. "Anything yet?" he gasped. "My arms are ready to drop off."

"Not yet; pump harder," she cried. "I want a drink."

"Thought you weren't going to drink?"

"Keep quiet and keep pumping."

"How about now?" panted Stix.

Ella bent her head upside down and looked into the spout. Splash! Woosh!

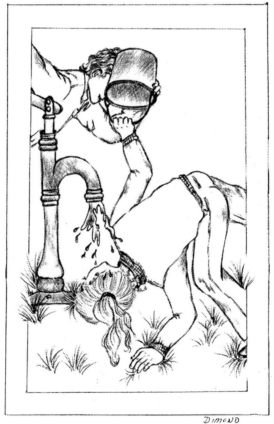

DIMOND

"Yowwwwwl!" she screamed. A slimy, greenish-brown water poured over her face and hair. She spit and sputtered. "Look at me," she groaned, shaking her head, her ponytail spraying water like a drenched puppy. "Oh, it smells terrible. And it's all your fault."

"My fault!" snapped Stix. "I wasn't the one who looked into the spout. You're the one that had to be nosy."

"Nosy!" wailed Ella. She glared at her brother, flopped down on the ground and began shivering. "Just look at me. Now I have to go home."

"No you don't." Stix handed Ella a handkerchief. "It's clean," he said, feeling a little sorry for his sister. "Dry off and we'll start walking again."

She wiped her face. "I need a towel."

"Oh, come on, don't be such a complainer." Stix tried to pull Ella to her feet. She resisted. "You look OK, let's get moving."

Ella looked up, brushing off the front of her jeans. "Is that all you can say?" Ella mimicked Stix, "you look OK?" Her lower lip curled over.

"Hey, you're not going to cry, are you?"

"Cry! Huh! Scream maybe, but not cry. But so what if I do cry? What would you do about it, Stix?" She forced a deep frown. "A girl has a right to cry if she wants, especially when her own brother says she only looks OK."

Stix slapped his forehead. "Now what are you saying?"

She sniffed. "I want to look more than just OK. OK is fair. OK is average. OK is OK for some people. For me . . . OK is the pits."

"What's wrong with being average?" Stix shrugged.

Ella grit her teeth. She dragged each word out just like Mrs. Kelly, the Principal, did when she was extra angry at one of the kids. "If yooooou want to be average, that's fine with me. If everyyyyyyyone in Figgsville wants to be average, that's fine with me. If the whooooole world wants to be average, that's fine with me. But I want to be more than just OK . . . Oooooook!"

Stix got the message. He knew there was only one way to get his sister moving. "Ella, you're more than OK. Believe me, you're very, very pretty and intelligent, too, even if you are my sister." He dropped his head and lifted his eyes ever so slightly, a tinge of pink brightened each cheek.

"Are you sure, Stix? I mean, you wouldn't lie about a thing like that, would you?"

"Naw, I mean it. You're much better than just OK."

Ella beamed with satisfaction. "Good!" She raised a hand toward her brother.

Stix pulled Ella to her feet. "Now let's get moving."

She kicked the dirt, spraying the back of Stix's shoes with little pebbles. "And I wasn't going to cry either." Stix shrugged and moved down the road.

After walking another mile on Old Route 99, Stix spotted a sign in the distance. "I think that's Felix's Apple Farm up ahead. You know . . . the one that dad always talks about."

Ella forgot her wet hair, "Beat you there." She took off like a rocket, calling over her shoulder, "Maybe we can buy an apple or some cider."

Stix eased the barn door open. It creaked loudly. The mouth-watering aroma of fresh apples tickled their nostrils. Cautiously, they walked inside. There were apples everywhere, Delicious apples in one pile, Macintosh in another and Granny Smith apples in a corner . . . all kinds of apples, piled higher than high.

Two ladies and a man stood by a wooden table, sorting, wrapping and packing them in boxes one at a time. Other than slightly raised eyebrows, they paid little attention to Stix or Ella.

"Can we buy an apple?" Ella asked cautiously, holding out her dollar. The man raised his ice-blue eyes. Wrinkling his forehead, he murmured under his breath and continued to pack apples, his arms moving in robot-like jerks.

"Sure am hungry," she said a little louder, dangling the dollar in front of one of the women, "I'm willing to pay." The lady handed her and Stix a large delicious apple and motioned for them to move on. "Don't you want paid?" The lady shook her head, continuing to wave Ella away. "But I'm willing to pay, you know. Really, I am."

Stix pulled his sister's arm. "Thanks," he said to the lady, then whispered to Ella, "let's go. Why pay for something she's giving away for nothing."

Ella's face lit up. "How about that, Stix? I made an impression on her. And that my dear brother," she mimicked his voice in an artificial low tone, "is because I'm more than just an OK person." She bent over and leaned her elbow on the table. "Don't you think so lady? Don't you think so mister?" Two apples rolled off the table and bounced off the man's foot. He raised his bushy eyebrows. He started to say something, but Ella quickly retrieved the apples and shoved them into his hands.

"Sorry about that."

One of the women rolled her eyes. "Better move along young lady before he gets angry."

"Oh sure lady, we're going. But I want to thank you for the apple."

"Yeah, yeah, yeah," grumbled the man.

Stix kept tugging at his sister's arm. Stumbling and tripping, Ella kept turning and hollering to the lady, "Thanks lady, thanks a lot. It's so nice of you to think of me as more than just an OK person." She waved her hand pertly in Stix's face and ambled outside.

Stix eased the door shut, muffling the woman's confused words, "What's she talkin' about, Sara?" the lady kept repeating to the other woman. "These kids nowadays are . . ."

After passing another barn, Stix suggested they turn around and head for home.

Ella grimaced. She leaned on a post and took off her sneakers. "I'm tired and my feet are burning," she moaned.

"You better not be too tired. See that sign, it says it's four miles back to town. Darn it, Ella, I warned you not to come with me. But no, you always get your way. Now what are we going to do?"

"I'll never make it." She rubbed her toes. "Look, I have a blister."

"Hummm." Stix spotted an old log. "Sit down and rest until you feel like walking again. It's still early." Stix flopped down beside her. *I'm glad she's tired,* he thought, *I can rest without her knowing that I'm tired, too.*

Ella wiggled her toes. "I'll bet you're as tired as I am, but I know you won't admit it."

Stix wiggled his toes inside his shoes. *I have a blister, too,* he thought, *but I'm not going to show Ella.* He tugged at his ear.

Ella spotted the canvas tips of her brother's shoe moving. "Bet you have a blister, too. You're just too proud to admit it."

Suddenly, Ella bolted to an upright position pointing to the other side of the road. "Look, here comes a bus! Let's take it. I have two dollars."

They crossed the road carefully. Stix waved, and Ella hollered. The driver slowed the bus and pulled over.

"This isn't a regular stop," called the driver over the hum of the engine. "But I guess you can get on."

"This enough?" Ella handed over the two dollars.

"Sure, and you get twenty cents change. It's half fare for kids."

The driver closed the door and slowly merged into the oncoming traffic. Ella and Stix wobbled down the aisle to the rear of the coach. "I get to sit by the window," Ella insisted.

"So what else is new? You always get your way." Stix sat quietly, moving his eyes from passenger to passenger. Ella knew something was bothering her brother because he kept tugging at his ear lobe. He always did that when he was puzzled or frightened.

"What's wrong?" asked Ella.

"Huh . . . ah . . . nothing. Nothing is wrong."

"Come on," insisted Ella. "You can't keep anything from me."

"What are you talking about?" Stix gave her a light jab with his elbow. "Keep your voice down. People are looking at us."

Ella wasn't the type to take kindly to hittin', pinchin', smackin', or jabbin' from anybody. Stix knew that all too well and he expected her to retaliate quickly, which she did. Whack! Ella slapped his leg. "Hands off bozo!" She shook her fist in his face.

"OK, OK," he grumbled, continuing to look at the passengers with a puzzled expression. Stix kept pulling on his ear until it turned bright red. "That's funny," he mumbled, fidgeting in his seat.

"Will you please tell me what's wrong?" Ella blurted out.

Several passengers turned to see what the commotion was about.

"Be quiet!" Stix said glaring at her. He lifted his finger, hiding it with his other hand and pointed to the men sitting in the seat across the aisle, then to a woman in the next seat up.

"What's so special about them?" whispered Ella.

"Look how they're dressed . . . suits, ties, and that's not an everyday dress that woman has on. Just like everybody else on this bus. And there are no kids, except for us."

Ella knelt on the seat. She scanned the bus, her head turning like a submarine periscope. "Wow!"

DIMOND

"You thinking what I'm thinking?" He pulled harder on his ear.

Ella looked bewildered. "The only time people get dressed up in Figgsville is for church."

"That's right, and this is only Tuesday." Stix lost his balance, sliding into the aisle as the bus turned onto the expressway ramp. He jumped back into his seat just in time to read the large, overhead road sign. Ella and Stix sunk back into the cushioned seats.

"Wrong bus!" they gasped together.

"We're heading for the city." Stix patted Ella's hand. "Don't be scared. We can take a bus back to Figgsville." He felt his pockets. "I'm sure I have two dollars. That should be plenty."

"Who's scared?" Ella's eyes lit up. "I think this is super-exciting. I've never been in the city."

"Yes you have," Stix reminded her.

"Don't be silly Stix, I mean by myself." She stared out the window, moving her head slightly with each passing car. "Just think, the city by myself," she sighed.

"Well, I'm with you," Stix said with a reassuring tone.

"Might as well be alone," she chortled, bouncing up and down on the seat. "This will be great." Her eyes glittered with excitement. "And it's not going to be booooorrring like Figgsville."

Stix, who was at first very worried, broke into a wide grin. "You're right. This could be fun. Not our fault we got on the wrong bus." They flopped back in their seats while the bus sped along the six lane expressway.

"To the city," Ella laughed, pointing straight ahead.

"Charge!" shouted Stix, his arm overhead as if he were holding a cavalry sword. "Away from old Figg-A-Figg-A-Do!" And again the passengers turned to see who was making all the commotion.

Ella wiggled her index finger toward Stix, nodding and smiling at the people. "You'll have to excuse him," she said coyly. "He's never been in the city before. Country folk, you know. Very excitable."

Stix rolled his eyes and fell back in his seat. "I don't believe it!"

Ella shook her finger at Stix, her face as hard as stone. "But it's true little brother."

"Who are you calling little brother?"

"Why you, of course. Now sit back and enjoy the ride. We are going to the city, and there is no need for you to worry. I'll take good care of you."

CHAPTER III

THE LOST QUARTERS

The bus jerked to a stop. Ella sat gazing through the window at the tall buildings. She barely heard the driver call, "Twenty-third Street."

"You think we ought to get off?" Ella asked, twisting her neck and dipping her chin, her eyes straining upward. "How high are those buildings?" Stix didn't answer. He too was staring at the people. Ella jabbed him in the ribs.

Stix flinched. "Hey, what's with you?"

"Didn't you hear me?"

"No."

"Are we going to stay on this bus forever?"

Stix pushed his nose flat against the window. "Don't worry about it," he said in a rather arrogant way. "I know where I'm going. I can remember everything about this place." He swung his shoulders away from Ella and continued to gaze out the window. "I'm a real city person at heart, like that kid." He jabbed at the glass. "Selling papers on a city street corner is better than cutting grass in Figgsville. Bet he meets a lot of important people."

"Twenty-eighth Street," called the driver, "last stop."

"So you know where we're going do you?" Ella gave a scolding sneer. "If we don't get off now, we'll be heading back to Figgsville."

The driver turned in his seat. "You kids gettin' off?"

They dashed up the aisle and bounced down the steps. Stix turned in the doorway. "Excuse me, sir. Can we get a bus to Figgsville . . . say about 4:00 this afternoon?"

The driver pointed to a wooden bench across the street. "Right over there. You can get one at 4:05."

"Is the fare the same?"

"Yep. A dollar and eighty cents."

"Thanks," called Ella.

"Sure thing." The door closed.

They were left standing at the curb in a cloud of foul-smelling diesel fumes. Ella held her nose. "I hate that smell, gives me a sick headache." A passer-by bumped her elbow, spinning Ella off balance. "Didn't even excuse herself. Rude person," Ella called after the woman who never turned for a second glance. Another woman bumped her from behind.

"You can't stand in the middle of the sidewalk like that. You're not in the country you know," the woman complained loudly.

"OK, OK!" Ella moved toward the bus stop bench where Stix sat counting his quarters, never noticing the bouquet of daisies that lay crunched in the corner of the wooden seat, half of which Stix was sitting upon.

"Two bucks on the nose. How much you got?"

"Twenty cents."

"We'll need $1.80 for return bus fare." Stix gave the quarters a quick second count. "Together we have an extra forty cents. Not much to play around with, not even enough to call home." Stix stuffed the quarters into his pocket and jingled them a bit. "Don't want to lose them. Come on, let's go do something." They flowed into the crowd and walked along gaping at skyscrapers, passing people, honking taxis, blinking lights and more people, all kinds of people, people who seemed to be going in all directions in one big hurry.

In front of an open-air market a group of men, dressed in dazzling white shirts and pants played Calypso music. They reminded Ella of a documentary she had seen on television about Jamaica. One man with a graying beard and several gold chains hanging about his neck beat on drums that looked like metal barrels with caved-in tops. His shoulders dipped with the beat, and he swayed gently at the hips. Another tapped four small, knobbed sticks against bulbs that resembled dried gourds. The smallest man strummed a giant guitar, and the leader sang and made clicking and snapping sounds with his mouth and teeth while playing a keyboard. A small crowd gathered. Some tapped their feet. Others snapped fingers and swayed from side to side. Stix could see that Ella was really getting with the beat. She swayed as she walked, her eyes fastened on the drummer's dancing hands. Dreamy-eyed, she sighed, "What a beat . . . yeah."

"Ella, look out!" bellowed Stix.

Ella barely had time to half turn her head when she walked smack into a well-dressed man who was carrying a briefcase. Splat! She spun around and grazed a woman toting three bags of groceries. Oranges plopped to the sidewalk. The woman reached out frantically trying to keep the fruit from rolling into the street. The other bag tipped, sending a stream of loose spaghetti and an endless line of cans zigzagging through the dodging pedestrians. The woman threw her arms up in despair, helplessly allowing the third bag to slowly slip away. Some items bounced off the concrete; others fell with a dull thud. Egg yolks oozed through the brown paper.

The man with the briefcase groped about on his hands and knees trying desperately to find his glasses, his tie dragged through the splattered eggs, his knees crunched the loose spaghetti. Just as he located the frames, a boy came whizzing through the crowd on a skateboard, heading straight for him.

"Look out!" Stix screamed.

The boy veered sharply to the right, desperately trying to avoid the man. Stix folded his arms over his squinting eyes, and so did the man. The boy pulled the skateboard up in a quick "wheelie", gave a grunt, then crashed smack into an outside market storage bin, sending a zillion walnuts, pecans, filberts and almonds spinning into the crowd. People slid, slipped and careened into one another while grabbing onto sleeves, coats, purses, shopping bags and whatever else they could manage to get a hand on until, one by one, they dragged each other into a heap of wavering arms and kicking feet. People on the bottom of the pile complained loudly of the pain being inflicted by the sharp, cracked nut shells.

"Why don't you watch where you're going?" scolded a woman who was laying in a puddle of sticky ketchup. An overripe banana rocked gently on her head. The man with the briefcase pointed to himself in disbelief, looking over his shoulder, hoping to find another person that she might have been talking to.

Dimond

"You don't think that I caused this mess?" He tried to explain and apologize, but the woman would hear none of it.

"Just look what you've done." She looked at herself in horror. "I'm bleeding!" she yelled.

"N . . . n . . . no ma'am, it's only ketchup." He gently removed the banana from the woman's head.

"Now you're trying to steal my banana," she scolded, shaking her finger in his face.

"Get off me," wailed another.

"But I tell you it wasn't me." The man scrambled to his feet. "Hey, there he goes."

The boy on the skateboard burst from beneath the pile of people.

"Aha! That's the one," yelled the store owner, pointing an accusing finger at the boy. "He's the culprit who caused all this trouble." People scampered to their feet. "Get him," urged the grocer. And away they went, chasing madly after the terrified skateboarder who tore through the crowd in flight for his life.

Through the mass confusion Stix and Ella slipped quietly away, mixing into another crowd of people who waited patiently for a traffic light to change at a busy intersection. They huddled together, glancing at each other out of the corner of their eyes.

"Don't turn around," Stix muttered.

"Are you kidding?" Ella practically dragged her brother across the street, making sure to remain in the midst of the crowd, which after a few blocks seemed to dwindle. Ella slowed, taking in the displays of the department store windows. Stix complained at first, until he spotted a window filled with a variety of sporting equipment.

"Oh Ella, did you ever see anything like it? Look at that neat tennis racquet and Ice Glider hockey stick. That first baseman's mitt is the . . ." Stix realized he was talking to himself. Ella was frozen to the glass a few windows back. "What's so interesting?" he called.

"Rainbow slacks and multi-colored sneakers," she sighed, "and look at that dress. I've never seen anything like it before in my life." She closed her eyes and took a deep, dreamy breath. "I wish that glass would disappear. Oh Stix, can't we just go in and look around for awhile?"

"What can we buy with forty cents?" Stix said, thinking about the hockey stick. "It would just be a temptation."

"What harm can looking do?" she asked with pleading eyes.

"You wouldn't listen even if I said no."

"You're right," Ella said with a grin. She started for the entrance, but Stix passed her in a streak, pushed his way through the revolving door and headed directly for the sporting goods department before Ella could take ten steps.

Ella breezed through the aisles. "This is like walking down fairy tale streets, ones lined with cotton candy dresses, soda pop tops, marshmallow shoes, jellyroll jeans and perfumes that smell so heavenly they make my nose tickle. I wish it would rain dollar bills."

Stix couldn't resist trying out the hockey stick. He eased it off the rack and gave it a few easy swings. "Awesome!" he said, taking a practice slapshot. On another rack there were a few loose, orange golf balls. *Must be for display only,* he thought, *that's why they're not in packages.* He figured the balls were also for testing putters, and maybe for trying out the Ice Glider hockey sticks. A few easy rollers wouldn't hurt anything.

The perfume test bottle was too much for Ella to resist. "Ummmm," she whispered, "an elegant bouquet made just for me."

The delicately lettered sign invited a sample spray: EXOTIC—A SCENT ONE CANNOT RESIST. She pointed the bottle toward the back of her ear. Crash! The bottle flew out of her hand, slid across the cashier's counter and landed in the lap of an exhausted saleslady who was taking a break. The cap snapped, and in the blink of an eye the woman was drenched in EXOTIC.

"Oh, no!" she screamed. "I'll never smell normal again."

Stix stared in disbelief. "All I wanted to do was give it a little nudge," he gasped, as the orange golf ball bounced over the cosmetic counter and came to rest at the feet of an angry security guard.

"Hey you," he growled. "Come here."

"Ooooooh!" Stix tore down the aisle, grabbed Ella by the arm and pulled her toward the revolving door. The security guard hopped over a counter in hot pursuit.

"Come back here!"

Shoppers were streaming through the revolving door so fast that Ella kept pulling back. "We're going to get stuck," she screeched.

Stix gave her arm a hard yank. "Come on, the guard's on our tail." They jammed into one compartment. The security guard pushed into the one behind them. Ella glanced quickly at the guard, his angry face pressed against the glass. He was beet red. Frightened, Ella gave an extra hard push on the door. It spun out of control, whizzing in circles so fast they couldn't step out.

After rotating four times the guard began hollering, "Stop pushing! I'm getting dizzy." But Stix and Ella were too scared to stop and pushed the door harder.

People gathered on both sides of the door, many of them laughing at the spinning chase. Five more quick turns and the security guard staggered out on the inside of the store, and the kids were thrust onto the sunbaked sidewalk. Stix did several tumbles into a mass of pedestrians, scattering them like bowling pins. An old woman shrieked as if she were in pain just as the quarters rolled out of his pocket, and one by one plunked through a steel grating that covered a loading shaft.

With clawing fingers Stix pulled himself to the darkened pit. He was so dizzy from the spinning door, he wasn't sure if he was facing up or down until he spotted a reflection of the last quarter still spinning on the bottom of the shaft. A crowd quickly gathered. Slowly he lifted his head. Ella was staring at him with dazed eyes.

"Jumping catfish," Stix groaned, "are we ever in trouble."

"How deep do you think it is?" asked Ella weakly.

Stix cupped his hands to block out the sun. He stuck his nose between the bars of the steel grate. "Deeper than the diving end of the Figgsville swimming pool," he gasped. He pulled on the grate but couldn't so much as budge it.

"You'll never pull it open," said a bystander who was pointing to the heavy padlock that dangled on the inside of the grate. "Do you want me to call the security guard?"

"Security Guard." Stix bounced to his feet. "Ah, no. No thanks. I'll take care of that." He felt the sweat forming on his brow.

"Oh yeah," groaned Ella, "you'll take care of it OK. How are we ever going to get home?"

They dusted themselves off, sat on a sidewalk bench and looked blindly at the grate-covered pit. Ella shook her head in hopeless despair.

Stix kept muttering, "There's got to be a way to get our quarters back."

"Maybe we ought to call Aunt Jenny, Stix."

"Are you crazy? You know how she is. She'd probably call the cops, or have one of her nervous attacks, besides we don't even have enough money for the phone call. Forget it, Ella. We just have to figure a way to get those quarters out of that pit."

"How?"

He looked at his sister with apologetic eyes. "I'm sorry, Ella. Honest I am."

"Forget it. It's both our faults," she said. "We wanted a little excitement, and we got it. Guess we should have stayed in Figgsville."

That angered Stix. "Look, we didn't exactly plan this trip. All we wanted to do was go for a long walk. And what was so wrong about that?" He paused, dropped his eyes and continued, "I'll find a way to get those quarters out of that hole." He propped his chin upon his hands and rested his elbows on his knees. "Even if I have to sit here all day."

"Oh, no you won't!" came an ugly, cackling cry.

DIMOND

CHAPTER IV

MATTIE AND HEDALGO

A strange looking woman with ice-blue eyes stood glaring at Ella and Stix. Her face was wrinkled and leathery and red as if it had been nipped by a frosty wind, even though it was the end of summer. She had a bouquet of crumpled daisies in her hand and wore a soiled baseball cap with "S-K" embroidered over the brim. A ragged, gray sweater partially covered a spotted, pink blouse which hung with the tails sticking out from behind. She leaned to one side, pulled the sweater back and rested her bony hand on her hip, crunching the daisies against a sagging, brown canvas belt. A pair of purple suspenders held up baggy camouflaged fatigue pants that rolled to folds of wrinkles just above an oversized pair of sneakers. A shaggy black and white dog sat perfectly erect at her side. He gave a few squeals and twisted his head from one side to the other, his tail swaying like a windshield wiper. The angry woman waved a bent umbrella with a threatening thrust toward the kids.

"Just who do you think you are buttin' in on my corner?"

"Your corner?" asked a bewildered Stix.

She tapped the umbrella furiously on the ground. "You better believe it's my corner, and I've got lots of witnesses to prove it."

Ella smirked. "Yeah, and I guess you live here, too."

"Better believe it," she thundered. "I sack out right over there." She pointed to an alley just beyond the steel grate that had swallowed Stix's quarters.

"You actually sleep in an alley?" Stix asked with a grimace.

"What's wrong with sleeping in an alley?" she hissed, the wrinkles at the ends of her eyes growing deeper.

"Everything!" Ella blurted. "Only hobos and bagladies live in alleys."

"Who you callin' a baglady?"

Stix tried to smooth over the remark. "I don't think my sister meant that. I mean, bagladies don't sell flowers."

"You apologizin'?"

"I guess so," Stix shrugged. He felt uneasy and fearful of the old woman.

"Speak for yourself," scolded Ella.

The woman pulled Stix aside. "You have more sense than that impolite, sassy scamp. Now why don't you be a good boy and just go away? And take your impish sister with you, too."

"Well, ah, you see, we can't leave just now. But we promise not to bother you," Stix said, shying away from the snapping umbrella.

Ella pushed forward. "What are you backing away from, Stix? You don't own this corner, lady. And what's your name anyway. I may want to report you to the proper authorities."

The woman's ice-blue eyes suddenly turned to bull-raging red. She twisted her mouth and grit her teeth. "May the rats of Higgin's sewer sic you both. Of all the nerve, and whatcha mean, you can't leave just now?"

Stix motioned toward the grate. "We have to . . ."

Ella slapped his hand down. "Shut Up! First thing you

know . . . this . . . this . . . whoever-she-is will cheat us out of our . . ." Ella bit her lip.

Stix caught on quickly. He almost blew it, and now Ella nearly did the same thing. He gulped, stuttering uncontrollably, unable to put two words together.

"What's the matter Stix?" Ella slapped him on the back. "Are you choking on something?"

"Na, na, nothings wrong. I'm not choking," he managed to say. "Just a little confused."

Ella slammed her foot on the pavement. "Look what you've done to my brother, lady. What's with you anyway?"

"Humph! What's with me, you say? I'm the one who should be askin' what's with you. You're the ones trespassing on my corner. Now move out before I really get angry."

Stix started to move away, but Ella stood firm. She said boldly, as if not hearing a word the lady said, "Are you really a baglady? I've heard about people like you."

"What's that supposed to mean?" the lady growled.

"Well, I guess I mean homeless."

"Like hobos, bums and bagladies?" the woman challenged, squinting her eyes and drawing her lips inward. In a low raspy voice she said, "Listen little girl, and I do mean little, because I'm homeless doesn't make me a derelict." Stix began mumbling an apology, but the woman cut him off short. "Just get off my corner or I'll, I'll, I'll." She swung her umbrella in menacing circles.

"Well look at her." Ella stuck her nose in the air, turned and gave the woman an uppity nod, ignoring her angry threats. "The least you can do is call us by our names. I'm Ella."

Stix moved swiftly behind his sister. Between the ranting woman and his defiant sister, he felt even more uneasy. "Don't tell her our last name," he cautioned Ella in a whisper. "You know what Dad says about talking to strangers."

"And this is Stix," Ella turned to her brother. "Why do you keep backing away, Stix?"

"Because he's got more sense than you," the lady grumbled. "That's why he's backin' away. He knows you don't belong here."

Ella started to open her mouth, then shut it, barely sidestepping the point of the woman's umbrella. "You wouldn't dare, lady. If you don't stop swinging that thing I'm going to call a policeman."

The word policeman froze the old woman in her tracks. She cringed, then looked up and said, "So what. If Officer Clicker is on duty he won't do anything to me. He's always trying to help the people who live around here. But he might want to know what you two are doing hangin' around a city street corner."

Ella didn't back off. "So what if he's not on duty? And even if he is, I might even call another cop."

The lady suddenly dropped her eyes and backed up a few steps. Stix sensed a moment of weakness. "Yeah," he agreed. "We'll call another cop."

"Now take it easy kids," the lady's voice quivered. She backed off some more, her hands extended as though she was pushing herself away. "I never hit anyone in my life, let alone a couple of kids. It's just my way." She looked more nervous as she spoke, the tone of her voice softened. "You wouldn't want to do that . . . ah . . . I mean call a cop." Then, trying to change the subject, she asked, "What did you say your names are?"

"Ella, and this is Stix."

"My name is Mattie. Now that we know each other's names won't you pleeeeease listen to me and get off my corner?"

Ella folded her arms stubbornly. "Seems to me you don't care much for policemen. Have you done something wrong?"

Trying to shy away from the argument, Stix wandered over to the grate. He stooped over and shaded his eyes, attempting to spot the reflection of at least one quarter. He wished that he and Ella could just leave and forget about the stupid corner, but he knew they had to get the quarters back first. At least that's what he told himself, but there was another reason that made him want to stay. It had to do with Mattie. Every time he looked at the old woman he felt things churning inside, things he couldn't understand or explain. He remembered his fantasy . . . how he wanted to meet new people . . . exciting people. First, he'd be afraid, and then he'd feel confused. He even thought he felt sorry for her. But he wasn't sure about that. A few times he wanted to laugh at the way she looked and acted. But he didn't dare. Stix looked back at his sister and the old woman. They were staring at each other with the oddest expressions. Words flashed through his mind: strangers . . . junkies . . . drunks . . . dangerous! However, as he gazed at the woman, the name baglady just didn't seem to fit, yet surely she was a street person, homeless and forgotten.

He wondered what the "S-K" on her hat meant.

Ella bent over and rubbed the black and white dog behind his ear. "What's his name?"

"Skags," said Mattie softly. The hard lines of her mouth momentarily gave way to a half smile. She glanced away, then turned with a stern glare, changing her expression in a flick of her finger. "Now beat it!" she snapped.

Ella sat beside the dog and put her arm around his neck. "This is a wonderful dog," she said softly, ignoring Mattie's demands. "You want to sell him?"

Stix cringed. *Ella is bent on getting us in hot water,* he thought.

"Enough is enough!" bellowed Mattie. "You're trespassing. First you steal my corner, and now you want my dog. Of all the nerve. Now get!"

"No." Ella gave another defiant look. "How can anyone steal a city street corner?"

"Go!" insisted the infuriated Mattie.

"No!" Ella countered firmly.

A tall policeman tapped a nearby fire hydrant with his nightstick. "Is there a problem here?"

Mattie quickly changed her tone. "Oh no, Officer Clicker," she said ever so sweetly. "We're just discussin' the politics of the city. I hear the politicians are going to run old Clicker for mayor." She forced a toothy smile, her leathery skin wrinkling in a thousand folds.

Clicker twisted his mouth into a wry smile. "Who are you trying to kid, Mattie? You better keep it cool, or I'll run you in for disturbing the peace or for parking your carcass in that alley."

"You wouldn't do that."

Stix knew that Mattie was pretending to shudder as she moved toward the alley. It seemed so obvious. *I'll bet this cop always acts tough toward her when strangers are around,* he thought. He watched Skags follow Mattie like a shadow. *What loyalty.*

Clicker turned to Ella and Stix. "Mattie bothering you?"

Ella shook her head. "Oh no, we were just passing the time of day."

The policeman seemed a bit surprised. "Do you know Mattie?"

"Sure," Ella answered quickly, her fingers crossed behind her back.

Stix stood on the grate in a daze. He couldn't believe his ears. One minute Ella was fighting and arguing with Mattie, calling her a baglady and being downright rude. Now she was protecting her, even lying about it, something she never did before; of that he was positive. His sister was a lot of things, but she was never a liar.

The policeman tipped his hat back with his nightstick. "So you know her, do you? Well I'd advise you not to be hanging around with Mattie and her dangerous pals." He bit his lower lip. Stix could see he was trying not to laugh. Clicker continued, "She's always getting into some kind of trouble. By the way, are you kids new around here?"

"Ah . . . in a way," Ella squeezed her fingers until her knuckles turned white. "But we know our way around. Got some relatives in the city."

"Are you sure?"

"Positively."

Stix turned away and rolled his eyes.

"OK. But if you need some help, I'll be around all day." Clicker walked away twirling the stick and whistling.

"Ella!" Stix nudged her in the back. "How could you lie like that? What's with you?"

"Big deal. All I wanted to do was keep her from getting into trouble," Ella answered.

"And just what does that mean? You've been giving her a bad time for the last ten minutes and hardly even know the woman. And now you want to protect her. Give me a break."

"I didn't start the trouble. She did."

Stix threw his hands in the air. "That's just the point, Ella. Mattie did start the trouble, so why are you protecting her?"

Mattie peeped around the alley corner. "He's gone," she said to Skags, creeping slowly forward along the wall. Skags followed cautiously in more of a cat-like creep than a dog-like prance.

Ella smiled at their approach. "I don't know, Stix. There's something about her. At first she really got me angry. Fighting with her is a real challenge, but there's something else about her, something fascinating. And I just love Skags. Anyone who owns a dog like him can't be all bad."

"Yeah, I know what you mean, and she certainly doesn't look dangerous to me. But she's still a stranger. We have to be careful." He glanced at the woman and sighed to himself, *Sure is a strange feeling.*

Mattie, now face to face with them, scowled. "Now look whatcha done, gettin' Clicker all riled up."

"What's with this Clicker guy?" Stix asked, shrugging his shoulders.

"A very special person, that's who. I ought to sic Skags on you both."

Ella burst out laughing, and Stix held his mouth. He didn't want to make Mattie more irritated. Things were getting out of hand, he feared.

"Whatcha laughin' at?" Mattie asked grumpily.

Ella knelt down in front of Skags. She stared at the little dog, patting his head gently. Skags nestled against her, moved his black, wet nose close to her cheek and gave a slurping lick. Ella said to her brother, "Can you imagine this ferocious little beast sicing us?"

"Get over here Skags," Mattie barked. Skags obeyed. "We must get this matter settled right now."

"Settle what matter?" Ella asked.

"Look, this is my corner. I got my rights, and I'm gonna prove it. Skags, you run and fetch Hedalgo."

Stix scratched his head. "This is getting complicated. Who's Hedalgo?"

Mattie folded her arms and squinted her eyes. She gave Stix the impression that she knew something they didn't. "He's the main man around here. Our people call him the Judge. Of course, you wouldn't know about that, not being from the city."

"How do you know we're not?" challenged Ella.

"Are you kiddin' me? Just look at those clothes, and listen to the way you talk. I'll bet you're from one of those country suburbs where the only excitement that ever happens is a once-a-year fancy Fourth of July parade or one of those silly school picnics. Wouldn't doubt it if you were from Figgsville."

Stix and Ella swallowed hard. "What's wrong with Figgsville?" they asked sheepishly.

"Ha, ha. Are you kiddin' me? Even the name sounds weird. Figgsville! What a bore." Mattie began laughing uncontrollably until Hedalgo tapped her on the shoulder.

"You requested my presence, my dear Mattie?" The huge man bowed and tipped a felt top hat with one hand. With the other he twisted his thin, sleek mustache. "Hedalgo, at your service."

DIMOND

The man appeared to be as wide as he was tall. He seemed as round in proportion as a basketball. Hedalgo was very dark skinned, and of all things, he wore a light blue tuxedo, the kind with long tails. He had on a stiff white shirt with pearl buttons down the front, and a navy blue cummerbund that matched his pointed, patent leather shoes. A slightly wilted pink carnation drooped from his lapel.

Stix walked slowly around the gentleman of the street, eyeing him repeatedly from head to toe. "Wow, you look great."

"Certainly," Hedalgo said with great dignity, adjusting his blue, velvet bow tie. "The Judge is a class act. I thank you for your most gracious compliment. But Hedalgo's time is limited, my good people. So what can I do for you?"

"These kids are treading on my territory. I told them to get, and they refuse to go." Mattie pointed an accusing finger at Ella. "And that one is down right nasty."

"Am not!"

"I demand a trial," declared Mattie.

"Sounds serious," said Hedalgo with great concern. "Surely a violation of the I-Got-Here-First, Juris-Junk-Code, Article nine twenty-five." He thumbed through a worn, black book.

"It is," Mattie assured him. "They're interfering with my flower sales."

"Flower sales?" blurted Ella. "What's she talking about?"

Mattie shook the wilted daisies angrily at Ella until the petals fell to the ground, then made a full curtsy to Hedalgo. "Your Honor, a trial, if you please."

Hedalgo pursed his lips and turned his stubby neck in a short nod. "So be it. I shall hold court in Flaggadoo's Alley."

"Court!" Stix shouted, then quieted as he glanced toward the corner from where the policeman had disappeared. "I don't think I'd like to go to court. I've never been arrested and don't figure on starting now." He pulled Ella back. "Don't be so quick to stick your nose in this mess," he cautioned her in an angry hush. "Let's think this over. We can't afford any more trouble than we already have."

Hedalgo gave a short teasing chuckle. "You two children must be from the country. That's just fine with me. But we're not in the country. This is the city, a very large city. And since we're not ordinary city people, we settle our disputes in Street Court. Fact is, we're not even ordinary street people; we're different, so we do things in different ways." He strutted toward Flaggadoo's Alley with an air of dignity about him. The others followed as though they were the subjects, and he was their king. Hedalgo pulled out a large, satin handkerchief, flapped it in the breeze, then laid it across an old, wooden box before he sat down. "Mattie, my dear, you must clean this place up if you expect me to hold Street Court here from now on."

"It's Flaggadoo, your Honor," she explained respectfully, dusting a garbage can lid off with her sweater sleeve. "He's been under the weather lately. It's that darn old arthritis, and he hasn't been eating well for months. Skags and I have been visiting him over at County Hospital." She slid the garbage can before Hedalgo. "He might be discharged today."

Stix saw Ella staring at Mattie. He knew she saw the sadness in her face as she talked about Flaggadoo, whoever he was.

"There's more to her than meets the eye," she whispered to Stix. "Maybe she's a softy . . . deep inside, I mean."

Hedalgo leaned forward, sighing heavily. "Flaggadoo's Alley is never the same without Flaggadoo's presence. It lacks a certain touch of class. There's an emptiness about the place." The judge reached into the inside pocket of his tails, withdrew a shiny walnut gavel, blew on the end, and banged on the garbage can lid. "I declare this court in session, the Honorable Judge Hedalgo presiding."

In the absence of Flaggadoo, who usually answered with a hardy "Here! Here!" Skags let out with a bark and shrill yelp.

"Ah, the wisdom of this little cur." He turned toward Stix and Ella. "That, my children, means Hedalgo's decision is final."

"Wanna back out?" Mattie challenged.

Stix and Ella faced each other with confused looks. Stix felt a bit light headed. So much seemed to be happening in such a short time. They whispered in each other's ear. "I'm not sure about this," said Stix. "Even though it's not a real court, how can we be sure we'll get a fair deal?"

Mattie overheard Stix. "Real court you say . . . Ha! You think I wanna get mixed up with cops? No way! This is a Street Court. Now if you don't trust the esteemed Hedalgo, you can just leave my corner, and it will be all over. Finished. You lose; I win."

Ella faced Hedalgo boldly. "Are you a real judge?" she asked firmly, but with a polite touch so as not to anger him.

Hedalgo snapped his coat sleeves forward with his meaty palms. "Certainly my child, graduated Juris Publico X-Distink-Quished. Yes indeed, graduated number one from the Uni-Varsity Of Pool-Cue-Tip, the one just outside Oxen-Ford, even spent some time at Eat-In, you know, the school the Brits brag about." He turned to Mattie and bowed deeply.

Mattie crossed her hands over her heart and looked to the sky. "Such an education," she sighed.

"Summa-Come-Loudly, I was. Even got me a Sheep's Paper Diploma." Hedalgo snapped his suspenders. "It's signed by the X-Cal-A-Bar Deanaroo himself, Mulligan Magin. The king was supposed to present me with special ribbons and other Distink-Quished award, except that, at the time, he was out of town on king business."

"Does all that mean you're honest, ah, your Honor?"

"Honest!" Hedalgo banged his gavel. "I, my dear child, am often consulted on the most difficult cases ever tried in the Su-Pree-Mee Court. Why even the mayor of this fine city Ex-Pelled my Sentence with a Veto to be his chief In-Terr-O-Ga-Tor."

"What's that mean?" Ella asked softly.

"Must be something good," Stix answered with a not-so-sure shrug.

Hedalgo bent forward and pulled a scroll from the garbage can, held it overhead and let it unwind. A bright blue ribbon and fancy gold seal snapped at Stix's shoes, who pulled back with a jerk before moving forward cautiously. The writing was so scratchy he couldn't read a word. Stix hunched over for a closer look. "That's some fancy ribbon."

"That it is my boy." Hedalgo inhaled deeply, thrusting his huge chest upward. He pointed to the scroll. "I'll have you know that is an O-Fish-Al-Seal. And rightly Note-Or-Iced by the judge of the Cream-In-All Court. Why every official in this city knows me personally." Skags barked in agreement.

"Quiet!" commanded Mattie. Skags squirmed between her shoes and lay with his head on his paws.

"What do you say?" Ella asked Stix, who stood rubbing his already reddened ear lobe.

Hedalgo banged a dent in the garbage can lid. "Shall we begin, my friends?"

Stix smiled. "Why not. What do we have to lose?"

"Only our bus fare home," Ella answered thoughtfully.

Hedalgo winked. Skags barked. For some strange reason Stix felt he could trust this peculiar looking street judge, and he knew Ella did, too. Something told him that they would be treated fairly. He glanced at Ella, who nodded approval.

CHAPTER V

THE STREET TRIAL

The kitchen fan from a nearby restaurant whined and squeaked, blowing warm air and scrumptious aromas of grilled hamburgers and onions through Flaggadoo's Alley. Skags lifted his twitching nose to the wind, his pink tongue hung limply from the side of his mouth.

Mixed sounds of a waitress calling orders, clanging dishes and a whistling busboy were suddenly swallowed up by the slam of a door.

High brick walls straddled the gutters on each side of humpy cobblestones, blocking the scorching afternoon sun. Other than the open stripe of blue sky overhead, Flaggadoo's Alley appeared as a city cavern, a tunneled courtroom. The shade, however, gave little relief from the day's heat.

Beads of sweat formed on Hedalgo's dark skinned forehead, yet he sat erect upon his throne-like box, his legs spread wide apart. One arm was folded across his knee. He held the gavel straight up with the end resting on the garbage can lid, patiently waiting for the stragglers, all street people, to find a place to sit or stand.

Among the spectators there was Anita the Recycler, pushing her rusted shopping cart with the ever-wiggling wheel zigzagging to and fro. Beside her sat Macho Muscles, who barely weighed one hundred and twenty pounds. Abdu Skins brought up the rear, twirling and spinning on red and white striped inline roller blades. "I'm ready," he sang. "And I'm steady." Abdu touched a pencil tip to his tongue and slipped a spiral pad from a hip pocket as he glided along. "Whatever they say, I'll write it my way. Mattie versus these kids." He scowled at Stix, who retreated two steps to allow Abdu to skate by. Abdu screeched to a toe-standing halt, raising his hands overhead. A quick spin sent his slicked-back, black hair in a frizz. Turning to Ella he announced in a threatening voice, "And you will be judged by Hedalgo the Whiz!"

"Wha, wha, whoopee! Bravo!" cried Anita the Recycler.

Hedalgo banged the gavel. "Take your seat, my man."

Abdu swung in a wide circle, turned on the speed, racing straight for Ella. She moved aside quickly, dipping below his outstretched arms as he performed a most graceful forward flip, landing on the lid of a trash dumpster in a perfect sitting position.

"Fantastic!" cried Stix. "What a super skater!"

Abdu Skins blew on his fingernails and polished each one briskly against his colorful satiny shirt.

Ella twisted her mouth in disgust. "How did all these people find out about this meeting?" she demanded, her eyes carefully examining each new person who passed by, except Abdu Skins, who she tried to ignore. His show-off antics angered her so.

"Trial, not meeting," Hedalgo corrected her.

Mattie delighted in Ella's anger. She sensed the confusion in her eyes. "You can tell this girl's not one of us, Your Honor." She bowed slightly toward Hedalgo. "The girl doesn't even know how quickly news travels on our city streets."

"Looks like a setup to me," said Ella.

"Aha! So that's what you think." Mattie pointed to Macho Muscles and Anita the Recycler. "You call them a setup? Oh no, little girl, not at all." She shook her head in such snappy jerks that the battered baseball cap tipped forward on her head nearly covering her right eye. She spun around to face the Judge, an air of triumph about her. "Insultin'! That's what it is, Your Honor, an outright insult, callin' our good friends a . . . a . . . a . . ."

Abdu skins quickly flipped the pages of his notebook. "Setup! I have it all right here," he declared proudly, tapping his pencil on the page. "That's exactly what she said."

"Jumping Catfish!" cried Stix. "He's writing down everything we say."

"You got it little man," Mattie assured him, "and the Judge just might not take kindly to your ugly Ac-cu-sa-tions. Isn't that how you say it?" She looked for Hedalgo's approval, who smiled with exalted satisfaction like a teacher who had just witnessed his prize student perform the most difficult of tasks.

Ella felt her stomach tighten. "Ridiculous, that's what this whole thing is. Silly! Stupid!" She began walking toward the main street. "Come on, Stix. We don't have to take this kind of stuff."

Abdu Skins jumped off the dumpster and skated in circles around her. "What's the matter? Is the little girl frightened of the street people?"

Ella stopped, turned in a jerk, and with her fists braced tightly against her hips, glared angrily at the skater. "Street people! Ha!" She pointed to his shirt. "I thought street people were supposed to be poor. Look at those skates. They must have cost at least fifty dollars."

Abdu turned to Hedalgo, a trace of guilt in his eyes and voice. "Your Judgeship," he said, rubbing the new, colorful shirt, "it's my new job. I'm really trying hard to fit in this special group, just like you said I should. The hot-dogs are selling big time. As far as the skates are concerned . . . well, my boss sprung for a loan. Everyone knows the old skates were worn through. And what would I be without skates?"

Hedalgo nodded. Macho sprung to his feet and extended his spindly arms. "Forgive him Lord for not sharing his new wealth with the Soup Kitchen."

"Oh I will," Abdu assured him. "I will, just as soon as I pay off the loan."

"Hal . . . hal . . . hallelujah!" shouted Anita. "That's what makes us special street people."

There was dead silence. Ella relaxed, then began walking toward the main street again. Stix followed.

"Come on back," Mattie called to Abdu Skins. "I knew she would back off. Just keep on going," she called after the kids. "And don't hang around my corner."

Ella stopped. She tightened her shoulders together until they nearly touched her ears. *She's bugging me on purpose,* Ella thought. Turning in a slow pivot she challenged, "Who said anything about backing off?"

Stix cringed. "Oh no! Come on, Ella," he pleaded, "let's get out of here."

Ignoring her brother's urges, Ella tramped back toward Mattie. When she passed Hedalgo, she smiled sweetly. "Just taking a breather, Your Honor."

"Ha!" Mattie scoffed, pacing impatiently before the Judge.

Hedalgo saw that Mattie was anxious to begin, but he didn't want to omit the opening ceremony. He pinched his chin, thrusting his lower lip forward. Slowly, he leaned backward, reaching into the rear of his box seat. With a flurry he snapped an American flag from a tightly rolled coil. He moved his head from side to side, his eyes searching the corners of the shadow darkened alley. "It wouldn't be right to begin without him," he said ruefully.

"I don't think Flaggadoo will be comin'," Mattie lamented.

"But I can't start the Street Court without a proper flag raising." Now the beads of sweat poured into Judge Hedalgo's bulging eyes. He fanned himself with the felt top hat.

"I'll do the honors," offered Mattie.

"Can't let you do that," ordered Hedalgo, "you being a main participant."

"Participant?" Mattie jerked her chin to the right. Skags turned his head to the left. Ella and Stix watched and listened in confused anticipation.

Hedalgo adjusted his tails and tugged on his wide lapels. "Excuse me," he said with a reassuring tone. "Since I know the law, particularly the ins and outs of street affairs, please let me explain." He pointed to Mattie. "You, my dear lady, are the plaintiff. And you," he thrust a stubby forefinger toward Ella and Stix, "are the defendants. But none of you, including my loyal friend, dear Skags, can raise this flag. Says so right here." The Judge pulled a black book from his coat pocket and began reading, "According to article 9, section 6 of the Super Street Trial Manual, the only person permitted to . . ." Suddenly Skags gave a wailing canine cry. He wagged his tail, barked and raced toward the street.

Hedalgo grumbled, visibly annoyed at Skag's interruption, but then he broke into a light smile. However, as the familiar shuffle and flapping of Flaggadoo's sneakers approached, every line in Hedalgo's face bowed upward. "Ah, my dear Flaggadoo. Welcome back!" Skags scooted in loops about Flaggadoo's legs.

Mattie scurried to help Flaggadoo to his favorite seat, a torn and battered stuffed chair with faded floral pattern. While doing so she brushed Macho Muscles to the side. "Move over," she ordered. "You OK, Flaggadoo?"

Nodding, he said, "Thank you, Mattie. I can make it." There was a feeble groan barely noticeable in Flaggadoo's raspy voice. Before sitting down, he took the flag from Hedalgo's hand and clipped it to a rope that was hanging from an overhead pole. Slowly he raised it. The Stars and Stripes flapped and waved in the breeze of the restaurant fan. Macho Muscles stood at attention; Abdu saluted and Anita bowed low.

DIMOND

Flaggadoo moved forward. All eyes were on him. As if in a solemn trance, he recited, "I'm pledgin' to this here flag, being an American and all. And for the public, includin' these good street people of this here beautiful city. And . . ." he turned toward Hedalgo, "especially to our esteemed Street Judge, for which we're all standin' or sittin', dependin' on whether one has a seat or not. Whatever the case, I do hereby certify that all people testifying today will tell the truth, the closest to the truth or be pitched into the depths of Higgin's sewer." He cast a cautious eye toward Ella and Stix, the forewarning evident in his raspy voice. "So . . . all being good citizens let this street trial begin, with liberty and justice, amen."

The street people echoed, "Aaaaaamen!"

Hedalgo banged the gavel. "Thank you, Flaggadoo. I feel much better now." He turned toward Mattie. "Let the trial begin. What is the charge?"

Under his breath, Stix mumbled, "We're finally going to find out what we did wrong."

Mattie tapped her umbrella in the direction of Ella and Stix. "Stealin' my street corner. That's the charge."

A groan came from the street people.

"Can you imagine?" whispered Anita.

"Unforgivable!" Macho Muscles declared, flexing his pea-sized biceps.

"Order!" barked Hedalgo. He grinned. "If you please."

Mattie paced back and forth, her arms folded behind her, the umbrella clutched tightly in her hand, bouncing her head in rhythm to her steps. "Oh yes, they're hangin' 'round my corner, disturbin' what little peace one might expect to have on a city street corner. And, of course, they totally crunched my flower sales."

"Excuse me!" shouted Ella.

"Out of order!" Abdu screamed.

Whack went the gavel. "Order in the court. Silence!" commanded Hedalgo. "Proceed Mattie."

Mattie smirked at Ella, then smiled at Hedalgo. "Now Your Honor, you know that flowers are symbols of love and friendship. Certainly they must be sold in a peaceful place, and that's what my corner was until these kids came along." She flashed an accusing glare in Ella's direction. "I asked them to leave a thousand times. They wouldn't. Now how am I supposed to sell flowers with them sittin' on my street bench?" She raised both hands to the street people begging approval. "Everyone here knows I store the daisies on that bench. And they go and sit on them. Crushed them, mind you."

"We did no such thing!" protested Ella.

"You'll have your chance to speak," Hedalgo assured her.

"But she's acting like we're common criminals."

Mattie ignored the remark. "You should have seen them, Judge. Crawlin' on the sidewalk like a couple of earthworms. Even caused a terrible ruckus in the department store. They got Clicker and the security guard all riled up. And he," she aimed the umbrella toward Stix, "tried to steal a hockey stick." Anita, Abdu and Macho groaned in harmony. "That's right folks, saw 'em with my own two eyes."

"Shoplifter is the word," called out Abdu Skins, busily writing in his notebook.

"Never!" shouted Stix. "I did no such thing."

"Order!" Hedalgo banged the gavel.

Mattie moved casually toward the Judge, fluttered her eyes, then turned with a most pitiful expression, dropped her head and faked a cry. "Sniff, sniff." Thinking no one was watching, she gave Skags a gentle nudge on the tail with her sneaker, the cue for him to play his role. The furry dog looked up and shrieked several ear-splitting howls, playing the part perfectly.

Ella rolled her eyes. "I saw that, but I don't believe it. Judge, she even has the dog trained."

"Yeah," Stix blurted. "She's faking it. We never hurt her or tried to steal her dumb old bench."

"I said nothing about stealing a bench," countered Mattie.

"I'm sorry," apologized Stix sarcastically. "But you know very well what I mean."

"No! What do you mean?" Mattie challenged.

"You know . . . about the flowers."

"So, now you admit sitting on my daisies."

Stix threw his arms up in frustration. "I didn't sit on your daisies," he screamed. "And how can you say a city street corner is peaceful?"

Mattie turned her back indignantly and continued. "Just look at this bouquet!" She shook the wilted flowers. Petals flaked to the ground. She thrust the remaining flowers into Anita the Recycler's face. "Whatcha think of these? Go ahead, give a whiff."

"N, n, n, no smell," Anita stammered.

"That's right!" boomed Mattie. "I can't sell no-smellin' flowers. Tell me, Abdu, would you buy them?"

"Never," Abdu said smugly. "I'm more of a fragrant posy lover. Besides, it looks as if someone sat on them." He glared at Stix, then quickly scribbled a few more notes.

"Exactly! And even if they smelled nice and fresh, people still wouldn't buy 'em. Not with those kids distractin' everyone. You understand, don't you Judge?" Mattie smiled delightfully at Hedalgo. "I must have my corner to myself so I can concentrate on sellin' flowers, fresh flowers, not ones that are sat upon. How else am I going to make a living? How else can I give my share to the Soup Kitchen? These kids are interferin'." Again, she shot an accusing finger at Stix. "It was peaceful until you and that sassy sister of yours came along." She folded her arms and pursed her lips. "I rest my case."

Hedalgo twirled the ends of his sleek mustache between his fingers. "Do you have witnesses, Mattie? You know, to prove that this is truly your corner."

"O, o, over here, Your Honor," squeaked Anita. "Mattie has been here longer than I."

Macho Muscles shook his head and flexed his spindly arms. "Her name is branded on the concrete."

Anita chuckled. "You brand cattle, Macho, not concrete. But you are right about Mattie. She's been with our group for ages. All the street people know this is her corner."

Ella pushed her way past Mattie. "I object! Vociferously, I object!"

Stix flinched. "Vo . . . who?" he asked dumbfounded.

"Where did you ever learn such a big word, and what do you know about objecting?"

"I've been watching 'The Judge' on TV."

Clang! The garbage lid vibrated from the whack of the gavel. "You're out of order there my boy. Only one should speak at a time." Hedalgo softened his voice. "Just what are you objecting about?" He leaned forward on the box, cupped his double chin in his stubby fingers and focused attention on Ella.

"These witnesses are all prejudiced. I mean they're all friends of Mattie."

"That's true, my child. But I believe they are still telling the truth. I, myself, see Mattie selling her flowers practically every day. And that's the way it is with us. We're not your ordinary street people, you know."

"What are you implying?" Ella mimicked Mattie by fluttering her extra long eyelashes.

Stix couldn't believe his sister's bold approach.

"I mean we cooperate with each other. We like to get along," explained Hedalgo. "It's a matter of sticking together, not like those gangs on the East Side or the shack bums along the tracks. We're good street people. It might sound strange to you, but it's true. Because we are homeless doesn't make us bad. True, we sometimes get into a bit of trouble. But for the most part we settle our own problems. That's what the street court is all about. And that's what he's all about." Hedalgo pointed to Flaggadoo. "He keeps us together, away from the others who have lost hope." Hedalgo cleared his throat and straightened in his chair, jutting his double chin forward with an air of dignity and pride. He declared, "But not one of us on the West Side has ever been in serious trouble." The street people applauded. Hedalgo stood, bowing low, acknowledging their appreciation.

"That's right," Abdu cried out. "There's no drugs or stealin' or cheatin' with us. We do our best to obey the law."

Ella turned quickly to the skater. "Oh yeah, then what did

that policeman, the one you call Clicker, mean when he said Mattie is always in trouble?"

Abdu jumped off the dumpster. "You would be in trouble, too, if you didn't have a place to sleep or eat or even go to the bathroom. It's not the kind of trouble you think. Like Hedalgo said, we're not like a lot of the other street people . . . no druggies or boozers around here. Maybe we're not perfect, but we try to get along. Clicker will even admit that, and he's a policeman." He raised his voice, "You two think about it. Would you be here right now if we were low-life derelicts?"

Macho Muscles gave Abdu a pat on the back. "You tell them, my man. They don't know what tough is like. Why don't you both go back to where you came from?"

"Yeah," added Anita. "And leave Mattie alone. All she's trying to do is survive and make some money for the Soup Kitchen."

Mattie dropped her head and sunk back. Stix noticed that she covered her face. Ella didn't answer. She couldn't find the words.

Hedalgo blew his nose in an ear-splitting honk and cleared his throat. "It's your turn," said the Judge.

Ella seemed to be frozen in her shoes. She continued to stare at Mattie. Her mouth moved but nothing came out. The Street People's words stunned her. They echoed through her mind like clanging cymbals.

Stix stepped forward. "I guess our only case is," he looked up at the flag, "based on Mr. Flaggadoo's stars and stripes." Determined to give a good pitch, Stix placed his hand over his heart and stood erect without flinching a muscle. "If you believe in America, then you have to believe that we have a right to sit on public benches and the right to walk on city street corners. We might be just kids, but Ella and I understand about freedom and democracy."

"Walking and sitting is one thing," argued Abdu. "But interfering with a person's business is something else."

"We didn't mean to cause such a problem. For one thing, neither of us meant to create confusion at the department store. And if it prevented people in any way from buying Mattie's flowers . . . well, I'm sorry about that, too."

Stix turned to Ella, whose anger had now melted into sadness. She was thinking about Mattie, and what it would be like to sleep in an alley in the winter. The thought of not having a bathroom was just too dreadful to imagine. And to not have a home . . . that was too awful for words."

"I think we better just tell the whole truth," she murmured to her brother.

Stix nodded in agreement and began telling the story of how they accidentally arrived in the city. "And then we stopped at Felix's Apple Farm . . ."

"Please skip the details, Stix." Ella continued to face Mattie, their eyes fastened on each other.

Stix told them about the bus and the department store, about the revolving door (Hedalgo snickered behind a closed hand), and about how the quarters fell out of his pocket and dropped through the sidewalk grate into the black pit. He told about Aunt Jenny and how she would worry, maybe even faint if she knew their whereabouts. At the mention of Aunt Jenny's name, Flaggadoo raised his eyebrows and mumbled, "I wonder. No it couldn't be."

"Did you say something Flaggadoo?" asked the Judge.

"No," replied Flaggadoo. "I'm sorry. It was nothing of importance."

Stix continued to tell of their predicament. Skags squealed softly as Stix spoke, almost as if he understood each word. "So, Your Judgeship, we can't leave this corner until we get our quarters back. Aunt Jenny is going to be worried sick. Really, it's not like we planned it to happen this way."

"That could take forever!" shouted Macho Muscles.

"The quarters are your problem." Abdu did a quick circle around Stix, his skates noisily thumping over the cobblestones.

Mattie raised her hand, hushing her friends. "I . . . ," She paused for a long moment. "I didn't know about the money. I mean, I heard this ruckus and even saw them crawlin' on the sidewalk, but I didn't see the quarters drop into the grate."

Hedalgo studied Ella's gloomy expression. She continued to stare at Mattie as she spoke, now remembering clearly the shrieking woman outside the department store. It was Mattie. She was sure of it.

"And what do you have to say, young lady?" asked the Judge.

Ella backed away with her head down. "Honest, Your Honor, we didn't know about the flowers. I can't remember sitting on them."

"Me neither," added Stix.

"And Mattie, do you still want the corner all to yourself?" Hedalgo asked. She didn't answer. The others waited quietly.

In the still of Flaggadoo's Alley the steady drone of the fan now sounded more like the distant whine of a siren in the night. It reminded Ella of when she was afraid of sirens, the horror of the endless, wailing sounds. And how Mom, Dad and even Stix seemed to understand. They never teased her about being frightened. "It's OK, Ella," her Mom would say, cuddling her close. She trembled just thinking about it. *How terrible it would be not to have a family!*

Ella faced the alley opening. She could barely see the edge of the grate. The quarters still seemed important. *After all,* she thought, *we have to get home.* But now she felt differently about Mattie and the others. What if Stix and she would have fallen into the hands of the Eastsiders? She knew now that these street people were different, much like regular folk in some ways, but so very different in others. Lately, she had been hearing so much about the homeless and poor. Reading about street people and seeing them on television was one thing, but this was something different. It was something she could see and feel.

Stix, like his sister, wondered how this group had managed to stick together. Often, he had seen pictures of bums and bagladies hanging around in groups, sleeping in cardboard boxes and roaming the river banks. He knew many of them might be dangerous. From the beginning he was leery of even being near Flaggadoo's Alley and the street people. Now something told him this wasn't the same. They all seemed so caring for each other, so alive and exiting.

Ella was considering her fights with Mattie. She now understood the old woman's anger. This wasn't just a battle over a street corner. For Mattie it was survival! A twinge of guilt stuck in her throat like a lump of gum. Her heart ached. Her eyes throbbed. Yet deep inside Ella felt there was more to the way Mattie acted, but she didn't know what it was.

Almost as if Mattie had read Ella's thoughts and felt her pain, she said, "Judge, I don't want to stop these kids from finding their way home." Her face hardened. "Mind you, I'm not looking for pity or sympathy or anything like that." But Ella and Stix now knew this was her way of putting on the tough act, even if she was a proud woman, determined to protect what little she had.

Hedalgo relaxed his grip on the gavel. The audience sat motionless. "Many of you have spoken for Mattie. Will anyone speak in behalf of Ella and Stix." He moved his head from person to person. No one spoke, except for two snappy barks from Skags, who wiggled between Ella and Stix and sat looking up at them. Again, the dog barked twice.

"Mattie," said Hedalgo, "seems your dog is trying to say something. Perhaps he has sided with the kids."

Skags howled and yelped as though he was presenting an argument to a jury.

Stix's mouth dropped open as Mattie came toward them, the umbrella thumping cane-like on the cobblestones with each step. A horrible thought flashed in his head. *Oh no, I was wrong. She is a violent person.* But Mattie only stooped to pet her dog. Skags licked his mistress's hand and leaped into her arms. Mattie faced Hedalgo. "Whatever you say, Your Honor. Your decision will be fine with me."

Hedalgo rose to his feet, snapping the wrinkles from his lapels and coat sleeves. "Well then, being of sound mind and healthy body," he bowed respectfully to Flaggadoo and tapped his stomach. "And having carefully considered section twenty-two hundred of the Animal In-Four-Ma-Tollogy Guide, I must pay strict attention to the actions of this unusual animal." He flicked a finger toward Skags.

"That skinny little runt!" squealed Anita.

Mucho Muscles shot to his feet. "Oh Anita, how could you say such a terrible thing about me?"

"Sit down!" Abdu ordered. "She's talking about the hound, not you."

"More than a hound." Hedalgo leaned forward as though he were talking directly to Skags. "This is a dog of hidden powers, a fair minded animal." Skags howled. "This dog understands people, maybe more than people understand people." Another howl drowned out the droning fan. "I think this dog can teach us all a lesson. He loves us for what we are, no matter what that might be. He even shows affection for the ones with whom his mistress has been at odds." Hedalgo pointed at Abdu. "And you my good man, you say the lost quarters are not your problem, and yet you say we are good people and that we take care of each other. Well now, what about these children? The only one to speak in their behalf is this little dog."

DIMOND

With his arms folded Hedalgo pronounced his judgment. "According to all street laws, including the Territorial Survivor Chapter, this corner belongs to Mattie. Rightfully so. But we, as good street people must also consider the Dog and Animal Rights Code. Ah, ah ahem." He quickly flipped through the black book. "That's section 101, article 2. Says here that any animal showing concern for the humankind is a creature of love and understanding. It therefore shall be our duty to take into account the feelings thereof in making street judgments. In other words folks, old Skags here likes the kids. So it is our duty to help them out."

Flaggadoo nodded. "It is our duty," he exclaimed.

Abdu quickly pointed to Anita. "She can do it."

"But, but, but Macho Muscles is better with kids," Anita barely mumbled, her lower lip quivering.

Macho Muscles turned to Flaggadoo, who stared directly at Mattie. *The eyes of a wise old owl are upon me,* thought Mattie. She knew her alley friend was telling her that she was the one that must help the kids. Secretly, she didn't mind it a bit. But she wasn't about to admit it openly.

"Everyone must help!" ordered Hedalgo. "Mattie, you may have your street corner back as soon as we can find a way to retrieve Ella and Stix's quarters."

"If you please, Your Honor," pleaded Mattie. "Since you're giving the order, let me be the one to help them." The others looked surprised, some totally shocked. But Ella and Stix turned to each other and smiled. "I'll ask if I need help."

"I told you she's a softy," Ella whispered to Stix.

"Humph!" grunted Mattie, the slightest twist of a smile at the edges of her lips. "It's the only way I'll get my corner back quickly and be rid of you both."

"Permission granted," pronounced Hedalgo. "Now I must be on my way. The closing ceremony, if you please kind sir."

Flaggadoo straightened his aching bones to as erect a position that he could manage. He saluted the flapping flag. "By the power In-Sta-Gated by me, and, of course, by our In-Tell-A-Gent, his Grace, the Judge of Street People, Hedalgo, who again has proven himself to be the sage of the streets, I do hereby close this Street Court, now and forever, hallelujah."

Macho Muscles hopped into Anita's cart. "Let's go bottle and can hunting," he said with folded arms.

"Ah, the sweet sound of jingling coins," sang the happy Recycler. "A nickel for us and a dime for the Soup Kitchen."

The clicking of Abdu's skates on the humpy cobblestones beat a snappy rhythm to the squeaking, wiggly shopping cart wheel and the low drone of the fan. Hedalgo whistled a lazy tune. Stix watched them disappear into the bustling crowd of pedestrians. He exclaimed, "And to think that just this morning I actually thought that life was boring."

CHAPTER VI

FLAGGADOO LENDS A HAND

Just as Mattie moved through the revolving door the
department store clock chimed. It was a large, old clock
decorated with twining stems and leaves made of copper. A
cherub capped with scrolls adorned each corner.

Mattie stopped momentarily, lifted her head and shaded
her eyes so she could see the large clock face. She spoke in a
near whisper. "Four o'clock. I feel so helpless."

Stix and Ella waited near the grate. They could tell by
Mattie's expression that the situation was hopeless.

"He wouldn't do it, kids," Mattie said.

Stix eased the wilted daisies from Mattie's hand, ushering
her toward the bus stop bench. "Sit down, Mattie. You look
exhausted."

They sat together on the bench watching the large minute
hand move slowly forward. "Three more minutes and the bus
leaves for Figgsville." Stix slid off the bench and began pacing
the sidewalk. "I knew the guard wouldn't help us remove the

grate. He's probably still angry about what happened. Can't say I blame him."

Mattie had tried everything to persuade the guard to unlock and help them lift the grate. He remained stern and uncooperative. "Why should I help those kids?" he had told her. "They nearly got me fired over that hockey stick fracas. And how about that little go-around in the revolving door?"

Mattie tried to persuade him by offering a fresh bouquet of flowers. "I'll bring one everyday for a week."

"What would I do with flowers?" he asked rudely.

"Take them home to your wife. She will surely love you all the more. Wouldn't it be a pleasant surprise?"

"Ha! It sure would, if I were married. But I'm not."

She remembered his flippant laugh. That's when Mattie gave up. The word *married* reminded her of a very sad time in her life. For years she and her handsome husband, Thomas, were so very happy. They had everything: a beautiful farm, animals, money, and most of all, they had each other. That was until Thomas died ten years ago. That's when her life crumbled. She wandered aimlessly; she squandered what money remained; finally, she sold her possessions and took to the city streets. It was a time of despair and loneliness. It was as though she was trapped in a world that didn't care. And neither did she. Mattie had run away to forget, away to the city, a place that she had seldom visited.

"Thank God for Flaggadoo!" she thought aloud. "Thank God for my special street friends! What would have ever happened to me had it not been for them?"

"What was that?" Ella asked, cupping her ear in an effort to understand Mattie's murmurs.

"Huh. Oh nothing," Mattie said, shaking her head to clear the cobwebs. "I must have dozed off."

It was now 4:10 P.M. A Red Arrow bus roared by, the destination posted and lighted above the windshield: FIGGSVILLE.

"It's five minutes late," Ella said.

"So what." Stix said with a sense of helplessness in his voice.

He was thinking about Aunt Jenny. He knew he had to call her. But how? Ella had twenty cents, and that wasn't even enough to make a local call. "Ella," he said, "if we don't call Aunt Jenny soon, I think she'll call the police."

Ella held out the two dimes. "Not enough. We should have found a way to call her when we first arrived in the city." Ella bit down hard on her lower lip. Stix rubbed his ear until it nearly turned purple.

"What a mess," he groaned. "There's no sense hanging around here. Now you can have the corner to yourself, Mattie. Come on Ella, let's get going."

"Thanks Mattie," Ella said. She moved closer and rested her head on Mattie's canvas belt. "I'm sorry about all the trouble we caused."

For the past two hours Mattie had tried desperately to mask her feeling for Ella and Stix. From the moment she saw them crawling on the sidewalk, Mattie knew they were in trouble. She never wanted to hurt them, but there were so many things for her to think about, things that weren't going well. Flaggadoo was in need of better treatment; the Soup Kitchen was in hot water with the landlord, and Hedalgo needed some bucks to help the new sisters on the block. Things weren't going very well for the old ladies. Their clothes were torn and dirty and neither of them had a bath in the last month. On the streets it was always a matter of priority, and for many, just plain survival.

Now things were different. Mattie had time to think about the kids. She wanted so much to help them, but it wasn't working out.

Through the street trial she fought to remain tough, a street woman with a cold heart. There was no place in her life for outsiders. Her only friends were the street people, Hedalgo, Abdu Skins and the rest. Flaggadoo was her only family, at least she considered him so. Long ago she vowed not to trust outsiders. Life was too cruel. She wasn't about to be hurt again.

Now she was exhausted. The trial was long, the security

guard uncaring. She failed Hedalgo and herself. The kids had missed the bus. And now this.

Tears welled in her eyes. Mattie fought to hold them back. "It wasn't you who caused the trouble, Ella. I'm the one who made such a mess of things," sniffed Mattie. She embraced Ella tenderly.

Stix choked and turned away. "Come on Ella, let's get moving."

"But where will you go?" Mattie asked.

"I don't know," Stix answered. He struggled to keep his voice from quivering.

"Maybe we'll find an alley like Flaggadoo's," Ella said.

"Yeah," agreed Stix, "I'd rather live in the streets than face the music. Anything is better than being grounded for a month." He bit down hard on his lip until it hurt, knowing he really didn't mean what he said. He felt so confused and angry, and so very worried about his sister.

"No!" Mattie snapped. The nasty hag-like voice returned. She hated her moment of weakness. *You can't let the children see how you feel,* she scolded herself. *No matter what they think of me.* "You'll do nothin' of the kind," she barked. "Both of you will stay right here on my corner."

Ella pulled away abruptly. "Who are you ordering around?"

"You, that's who." Mattie picked up her umbrella from the bench and snapped it at Ella's feet. "Now sit down!"

"I won't" cried Ella, squinting her eyes, a pert look about her. "First you try to kick us off your corner, now you're ordering us to stay. What's with you, Mattie?"

"Never you mind. Just stay on the corner until I get back."

"I won't"

"You will," demanded Mattie.

"What's the matter, Mattie. You afraid we'll give you a little competition?"

"What's that supposed to mean?"

Ella gave her a saucy stare. "Maybe we'll sell flowers on the next street corner."

"You two wouldn't survive the real streets for more than a

night. Bums, hobos, drunks, thieves. God knows what else is
out there. Flaggadoo's Alley is different. It's like a haven for
the homeless, a place you won't find anywhere else in this city.
And besides, you can't be runnin' away from your problems."

"Look who's talking." Ella grabbed her mouth.

The remark hurt Mattie, but it was the truth, and she knew
it. The trick was not to let the kids know how she felt. Somehow
she had to prevent them from wandering off on their own.
She knew the dangers of the streets, especially the East Side.
Mattie grit her teeth. "Of all the sassy little imps."

"Oh no," groaned Stix, slapping his forehead. "Here we go
again." The bickering grew louder and more threatening just
as it had been a few hours before. It's what Mattie wanted . . . to
keep Ella and Stix busy until she could find a way to get them
home. But she also knew she needed help.

Passerbys stopped and watched the raging argument. Some
people took Ella's side; others sided with Mattie. Some groaned;
some laughed. One guy took bets on a winner. "I'll give two to
one odds on the baglady," he yelled.

"Watch who you're calling a baglady," scolded Ella.

"I'll fight my own battles if you please," Mattie demanded
gruffly.

"Don't be so bossy," said Ella, "You're just like our Aunt
Jenny."

Stix backed away, slumping on the bench. *If only I had those
quarters*, he wished. *What are we going to do?*

From behind an old refrigerator box that leaned half
bent against the alley dumpster, Flaggadoo secretly watched
and listened. He raised his eyes and whispered in a throaty
voice, "Aunt Jenny . . . hum . . . I wonder . . . could it be?"
He poked through the crumpled shopping bag that he
carried everywhere with him. At the bottom he felt a round
plastic container. Carefully, he removed the taped lid and
twirled his finger through the mix of pennies and nickels.
"That should do it," he said, replacing the lid and slipping
the container into the pocket of his torn sweater. He waited

patiently for a cluster of pedestrians to pass, then mingled with the crowd, shuffling slowly from the alley to the bus stop bench.

"You still here?" he said, pretending to be surprised. At the sight of Flaggadoo all squabbling ceased. People immediately lost interest and quickly moved on their way.

"Good afternoon, Mr. Flaggadoo," greeted Ella with a forced smile.

"Well it is for me, Ella," he said. "But it doesn't seem to be for you." He turned to Mattie. "Why aren't they on the bus?"

Mattie dropped her head. "I couldn't help them, not because I didn't try mind you." Motioning the umbrella toward the greedy grate, she said, "The quarters are still in the pit. Please don't tell Hedalgo I failed." She turned to Ella. "But I haven't given up yet," she said sternly. "It's just that I have to convince this stubborn little one to stick around until I come up with another idea."

"Who you calling stubborn?" shrieked Ella.

"You, that's who. Now you listen to me."

"Hold it!" Stix screamed, jumping off the bench. "Please Mr. Flaggadoo, make them stop." He explained what had happened, providing all the details. "And as you can see, we really have a problem. Honestly, Mattie it's not your fault that we're not on our way to Figgsville."

"Figgsville!" Flaggadoo broke into a broad smile. Now he knew for sure who Aunt Jenny was. He straightened his curved spine and thrust out his hand to Stix. "Put it there my friend. It's so nice to meet someone from good old Figgsville. I had no idea you kids were from my old hometown."

Stix extended a limp hand. His mouth agape, he uttered in surprise, "You're from Figgsville?"

"At one time I was," said Flaggadoo. "That was long ago of course." He gazed dreamily at the sky. "Ah, what wonderful memories. I can recall playing cards on the American Legion porch. Tell me, does that red-faced Charlie Honkers still have a double chin?"

"You mean the man that never wins at cards?" asked Stix.

"That's him all right, never could play Gin Rummy. At one

time old Charlie and I were the best of friends." Flaggadoo sat on the bench, crossed his knees and leaned back with his arms outstretched on the back rail. "I can remember when Charlie and I joined the school band with Jeddy Parkins."

"Jeddy Parkins . . . naw, he's too young," Stix said to Ella.

Ella flopped down beside Flaggadoo. "I'll bet it was his dad, Stix. Isn't that right, Mr. Flaggadoo? It just has to be his dad. Everyone in the Parkins family loves music. Jeddy is always playing his stereo."

"I suppose so." Flaggadoo rubbed his chin. "I kind of remember someone saying he had a son."

"Tell me, Mr. Flaggadoo, did you leave Figgsville because it was a dull town?" Stix grinned at Ella. But when Flaggadoo said it wasn't, and that he found Figgsville exciting and an interesting place, both Ella and Stix stared wide-eyed at the old man. "Then why did you leave?" they both asked.

"That's a long story. Right now, I think there is a more pressing issue at hand. Don't you think it's time you call your Aunt? What did you say her name is?"

"Jenny," Stix said.

Ella held out the two dimes. "We don't have enough money for the phone call."

While she spoke, Flaggadoo opened the plastic container. He poured a handful of coins into Ella's palm. "Wish it was enough to pay your bus fares."

"We can't take your money," she said. Stix bumped her with his knee.

Flaggadoo dropped another ten pennies into Ella's opened hand. "We'll just call it a loan."

"Thank you," she said, turning to Stix. "I think you better call."

"I guess I better. I wish I knew what to say."

"You might start by telling her the truth, like you did at the street trial." Flaggadoo pointed across the street. "There's a variety store. Change the pennies for nickels and dimes. Mattie and I will meet you at the corner by the public telephone."

Stix swallowed hard as the man in the variety store counted out fifty-five cents. "This isn't going to be easy," he said to his sister. "I hope Aunt Jenny doesn't pass out when I tell her where we are."

"Don't worry Stix," answered Ella, "she'll be too angry to faint."

DIAMOND

CHAPTER VII

THE BUBBLE GUM STICK

Stix tapped each number as though the push buttons were red hot. He visualized Aunt Jenny screaming into the phone. Sweat rolled off the end of his nose. Suddenly, he slammed the receiver onto the hook, thrust his head against the metal phone box, and stood motionless staring at the ground. His quarter jingled into the coin return.

Flaggadoo placed his arm on Stix's shoulder. The boy backed away just enough to allow Flaggadoo to retrieve the quarter. "Pick up the phone, Stix." Flaggadoo spoke in a gentle but firm tone. "Try it again," he urged, reaching to reinsert the coin. "You have two more quarters, so don't be in a hurry."

Stix turned momentarily to face Ella and Mattie. They smiled, and Flaggadoo nodded to show his support.

On the first ring Aunt Jenny answered. "Collins's residence."

"Hi Aunt Jenny," Stix said in a near whisper.

"Hello Stix," she said cheerfully. "The ladies just went

home. We had a wonderful afternoon. My strawberry jelly roll came out perfect. And for once everyone showed up on time."

Stix covered the receiver. "Ella, we're in luck. I forgot. This is Aunt Jenny's bridge club day. I'll bet she hasn't even begun to make dinner."

"We had such a delightful time," Aunt Jenny continued. "You should have seen the ridiculous hat Mabelline Frecas had on. My goodness, I wouldn't wear such a silly thing to a circus parade. Hum, come to think of it, she looked more like a clown than a woman. And Lillian Bushinberry wore . . . say . . . why are you calling?" Her voice suddenly increased in volume. "Is there something wrong?"

"Oh no, nothing's wrong!" Flaggadoo frowned. Mattie shook her finger and tapped her umbrella. Ella poked him in the small of his back. "Ow!"

"What's that!" asked Aunt Jenny. "Are you sure there's nothing wrong? Where are you? What are you doing? Where's Ella?"

"Get on with it, Stix," whispered Ella.

Stix stammered. "Wh, wh, where am, am, am I? Now that's a good question. By the way, Aunt Jenny, who won the bridge game?"

"Stix, is there something you're not telling me?"

"Well . . ." Stix hesitated. "We do have a slight problem. No emergency or anything like that, so don't get upset."

"Aha!" she bellowed.

Stix jerked the phone away from his ear.

"I knew something was wrong. Ella . . . that's it. Is Ella hurt? Because if she is young man, I'll see to it that your mother and father . . ."

Stix buried the receiver in his chest. "I knew it," he groaned as if in great pain. "I haven't even told her anything yet, and she's already having a fit." Each time he put the phone to his ear Aunt Jenny's ranting stung their ears like a blast of aerial fireworks.

Flaggadoo reached for the phone and muffled it with the

palm of his calloused hand. "Be more aggressive. Tell her where you are." He extended the receiver to Stix, patting him softly on the shoulder.

"Aunt Jenny!" Stix raised his voice. It did little to quiet her.

"You're not going to be late for supper are you? Six o'clock sharp, that's what time I want you home, and if you're one minute late no dessert, no TV, no computer games, no nothing."

"Aunt Jenny!" Stix yelled directly into the receiver. There was a long silence.

"My goodness, Stix, you don't have to break my eardrum." Aunt Jenny scolded, "Can't you speak in a civilized tone of voice."

Ella heard every word, and she couldn't hold back. She turned away to snicker with both hands clasped tightly over her mouth. "Can you believe it?" she said to Mattie. "She, of all people, wants Stix to speak softer."

"Yes, Aunt Jenny, is this better?" Stix's voice was almost maple sugar sweet. "Like I was saying, we started out taking a walk, and before we realized it . . ." Stix went on and on, explaining their adventures on old Route 99. "And like I said, we have a slight problem. You see, we ended up on the wrong bus." He tried desperately to explain. "It was a mistake. Really Aunt Jenny, we were very tired, and Ella saw this bus coming, so we got on, thinking it was going to Figgsville. But as it turned out we ended up in ah, in . . ."

"Where did you say you are?" bellowed Aunt Jenny.

"In the city," Stix answered in a near whisper.

"The City! Heaven help me! I think I'm going to faint."

Stix twisted his face in a most painful contortion. "I knew it. I knew it."

Flaggadoo eased the phone from Stix's sweaty hand. "Hi Jenny, this is your old friend Flaggadoo. Remember me?" There was silence. Flaggadoo knew she would be dumbfounded.

"What's he saying?" Stix mumbled. Ella shrugged.

"Flag-ga-doo," Aunt Jenny gasped, dragging out each

syllable. "Fin-i-gus Fer-din-and-o Flag-ga-doo?" Jenny sighed deeply. "I must be dreaming. It couldn't possibly be."

"Yes Jenny, it's me. And I'm with Stix and Ella." He heard her gasping uncontrollably.

"Who is this?" she managed to say, her voice filled with doubt and suspicion, demanding an instant explanation.

"Flaggadoo, you're old childhood sweetheart."

Ella and Stix stared bug-eyed at each other. Nobody said a word for what seemed an eternity. The sounds of the city smothered them: screeching brakes, roaring diesel engines, honking horns, a siren and a mix of a million voices of the rush hour passing pedestrians. "Get your evenin' paper!" called a dirty-faced urchin.

The faint call of Abdu Skins came from the opposite side of the street, "Hot-dogs! Lemonade!" The choking odor of exhaust fumes lay heavy on the streets.

"I get it," said Aunt Jenny. "Stix, have you been kidnapped? Who is that man, the one who said he's Flaggadoo?"

"It's me, Jenny, believe me, it's me . . . Flaggadoo."

"Prove it."

"That's easy. Tell me, do you still have your majorette uniform, the one with the blue collar embroidered with gold. And your gasping and wheezing isn't new to me. I know all about those asthma and allergy attacks. If it isn't excitement that sets you off, it's a fluffy cat or ragweed." Jenny remained quiet, more from shock than from curiosity. Whatever the case, it gave Flaggadoo the time to explain what had happened in great detail. Jenny listened closely, gasping and panting at each turn of events.

"There's nothing to worry about, Jenny. The children are in good hands. You know you can trust me."

"Your time is up," interrupted the operator. "Please deposit twenty-five cents."

Flaggadoo motioned for Stix to deposit another quarter. He held up the last quarter to remind Flaggadoo that the time was limited.

"Jenny, we only have a few more minutes to talk, so I want you to listen closely. The kids are just fine. There's a bus to Figgsville at 9:05. I'll see to it that Ella and Stix are on it." Mattie cringed. "There's absolutely no reason to worry, so don't be calling the police or doing anything foolish. I'll get them both home."

"Oh Flaggadoo, I'm so confused. Are you sure everything will be all right?"

"My word of honor," Flaggadoo promised. "If anything changes I'll call you immediately."

So many questions came to Jenny's mind: How did Ella and Stix ever meet Flaggadoo? Where does Flaggadoo live? Will they have something to eat? Are they really safe? She heard Mattie's voice in the background.

"Is that your wife, Flaggadoo?" Aunt Jenny asked.

"No," he answered. "Just family, Jenny, just family."

"Please Flaggadoo, take care of the children."

"Believe me, Jenny, everything will be just fine. I have to go now. Yes Jenny, I'll call. Yes, I'm just fine. Very successful, healthy and happy." Flaggadoo hung up and struggled toward the bench. He sat down in the corner and flung his neck backward with his eyes closed. His knees and hips pounded with pain. "It's the punishment for telling white lies," he murmured.

Mattie sat beside him. "Oh Flaggadoo, my Flaggadoo, you're too good of a person to be punished. It's your arthritis flaring up. You're supposed to rest. You know what the doctor said."

"But I promised Jenny that I'd have the kids on the 9:05 P.M. express to Figgsville."

"You relax," ordered Mattie. "I have a good idea. We'll raise the money for their bus fare, and maybe, just maybe, we will have a great time doing it. You kids stay here with Flaggadoo. I've got to go and find Hedalgo."

Ella started to say something, but Stix was quick to grasp her mouth. He faced his sister nose to nose. "Not now, Ella. Cool it!"

She gave a faint wave and smiled. Stix let up on his grip, but not before Ella gave him a hard jab to his ribs with her elbow.

No sooner had Mattie disappeared around the corner, when Abdu Skins skated by pushing a small food cart, which had large spoked wheels. It was painted candy apple red trimmed with yellow stripes. Along each side, fancy western style letters read: HOT-DOGS—POPCORN—LEMONADE. He parked the cart on the sidewalk next to the bench on which Flaggadoo and the kids were sitting, popped up a large umbrella that shaded the steaming dogs and placed a special vendor's hat on the back of his head. The aroma of hot-dogs and popcorn filled the air. Ella closed her eyes and licked her lips. Abdu heard Stix's stomach growl.

"Hey, you kids are hungry. And Flaggadoo, you look a bit pale. When's the last time you ate?"

"I can't remember," he answered, slouching lower on the bench. He didn't know which was worse, the pain in his joints or the burning in his stomach. The doctor had ordered him to take the new medicine three times a day and to eat before each dose. He thought the advice was amusing. With the Soup Kitchen temporarily out of business, he was lucky to eat once every two days. Even when times were good he seldom ate more than one meal a day.

"Something has to be done about that," declared Abdu Skins. "I'll make each of you a dog and an ade."

Ella smiled from ear to ear, then quickly frowned as Flaggadoo firmly announced that although he was extra hungry, there was no way that he would accept food without payment.

"Besides," he said to Abdu, "you have a loan to pay off. Giving away food will just get you deeper in debt."

Abdu knew better than to argue the point with Flaggadoo. The old man seldom accepted charity. "Well, how about you kids? Do you want yours with or without chili?" Stix rubbed his stomach. It growled louder.

Ella held out her two dimes. "What can I get for these."

"Don't worry about the money," said Abdu. "You can pay me anytime."

Ella was tempted to take him up on the offer. But she knew that the chances of seeing Abdu again were very slim. She glanced at Flaggadoo, who now had his eyes closed, an awful expression on his face, his skin ashen and clammy. "Can you give Mr. Flaggadoo a cup of lemonade."

Abdu rubbed his chin. "Sure, but he won't drink it. I know him too well. He only takes what he can pay for. I think that's the reason he's always sick. The man doesn't eat right."

"Mr. Flaggadoo!" Ella gave the old man a shake. "Where's your money box?" He slid it across the bench. She took off the lid. "It's empty."

"You gave us all your money for the telephone call." Stix said, his voice hinting shame, his heart aching with mixed feelings of anger and sympathy. "How are you going to eat?" His stomach gave another growl. It made him think of his own hunger and how Ella must be feeling. "What a bummer."

"What can I buy for twenty cents?" asked Ella.

Abdu Skins unscrewed the fishbowl-like jar on the cart counter. "Four pieces of bubble gum, that's the best I can do."

"I'll take them," Ella said, handing over the dimes.

"But I don't want your money."

Stix looked at Ella and Flaggadoo. "Sorry Abdu, I know how my sister feels. You might as well take the money."

Ella unwrapped a piece of bubble gum and gave it to Flaggadoo. "Maybe it will help take away the hunger pains."

Gently, Flaggadoo took her hand and folded her fingers over the gum. "Thank you, Ella. You're very kind, but I'm afraid my teeth won't cooperate. They're not working so good lately."

"That's it," Stix cried, scurrying to the greedy grate. "Bubble Gum! Come on Ella, chew it as fast as possible, and give me some, too. Abdu," he called over his shoulder, "Where can I find a long, thin stick?"

Flaggadoo's eyes snapped open. He danced toward Stix with a slight limp. Crowsfeet formed at the corners of his eyes as be broke into a watermelon-slice smile. "What a great idea," he whistled. "Quick, Abdu, go to the alley and fetch the flag pole. I'll mind your food cart."

Stix and Ella chewed the bubble gum into tight, sticky

chunks. They wound each wad around the end of the thin flag pole, and carefully lowered it into the dark pit. The sun, now lower in the sky, make it much easier to spot the quarters.

Ella counted, "One, two, three, and there's one over in the corner."

"Five, six, seven, eight," Stix paused, then blurted, "nine! Hey, we only had two dollars, that's eight quarters."

"Yeah." Ella agreed, "Where did the ninth one come from?"

Stix plunged the sticky gum directly on one of the coins. "I don't know, Ella, but I'm going to try and bring them all up, one at a time." He pressed the pole down then gently raised it up. The coin stuck firm. Stix lifted the pole a little at a time. When the gum was just under the steel grate, Ella squeezed her fingers under the quarter and helped guide it through one of the holes.

Stix pulled the quarter from the gum and raised it into the air. "I've got it! I've got it!" Ella, Flaggadoo and Abdu gave a cheer.

One by one, they raised the coins with the sticky pickup tool. The ninth one was a dime. Ella made a quick count. "Two dollars and ten cents, more than enough to pay for our bus fare. Stix, you're a genius. Too bad you didn't think of the bubble gum idea before the bus departed. We could have been home by now."

Stix smiled with great satisfaction. "I guess it was a pretty good idea, but I would never have thought of it if you hadn't bought the bubble gum from Abdu Skins." Stix slipped the money into his side pocket, jingling it carefully with his hand. He twisted a handkerchief around the coins. "I'm not going to lose them this time." He jumped up and down to show Ella the coins were stashed safely in the bottom of his pocket.

Ella jumped beside Stix. Soon they were twirling in circles. Abdu joined in, and Flaggadoo, without thinking about his arthritis, took to dancing a few steps.

Flaggadoo came to an abrupt stop. Clutching his right knee, he groaned. Abdu and Stix took him by the arms and helped him back to the bench. Flaggadoo breathed deeply as he eased himself into the corner of the bench, his eyelids drooping. He looked quite pale. Even his lips seemed more blue than pink.

Stix turned away and bit his lower lip. Ella swung around and took her brother's hand. They searched each other's eyes, their thoughts transmitted in expressions, their feelings mutual, knowing each other's heart. The decision had been made.

Stix took the money out of his pocket. The aroma of grilled hot-dogs caught the summer breeze. Ella inhaled. "Gosh, that's better than Aunt Jenny's pot roast," she said, licking her lips. Stix's stomach gave another growl.

"How much for three hot-dogs and three lemonades," he asked Abdu Skins.

"Seventy cents will buy one dog and a medium ade."

Another Red Arrow bus roared by. Stix watched it merge into traffic, then he turned to Ella, gazing at her with a painful frown.

"Go for it!" She said with a smile that accented her approval. "I'm dying of hunger. I've got to eat. Now!"

"I'll take three of each, that is, if you're not hungry, Abdu," said Stix, his face now lighted with a grin.

Abdu skated to the food cart.

> "Don't worry about me.
> I eat free, you see.
> Dogs are my pay,
> up to three a day,
> with cold lemonade.
> I've got it made."

He laughed and quickly jotted down his rhyme, then served up the dogs, adding a generous portion of chili to each one.

Flaggadoo protested, "You can't spend the money on food. It's your bus fare."

"Maybe so," Stix added onions to one of the steaming hot-dogs served by Abdu, "but right now eating is more important than riding on a bus."

"You can still owe me the money," offered Abdu.

"No," Ella said, serving one of the hot-dogs and lemonades to Flaggadoo. "We'll pay for everything now."

"Hold it!" ordered Flaggadoo. "I don't accept handouts."

"Who said anything about handouts," countered Ella. She winked at her brother. "We're just going to pay back the money you loaned us for the telephone call to Aunt Jenny."

Stix counted out $2.10. "Just right. Good thing we found that extra dime." He chomped on the dog. "Maybe our luck is beginning to change."

"I know it will," said Ella. "Mattie will think of a way to get us home."

"I sure hope so," Flaggadoo managed to say between bites and slurps. "I sure hope so."

CHAPTER VIII

THE JAMAICAN STREET JUMBLE

Hedalgo walked in circles at the entrance of Flaggadoo's Alley barking rapid-fire orders to the street people. "Stretch the sign a bit more. That's it, Macho. Now take the sag out of the center. C'mon, we've done this a hundred times. It should come easy to you now." Hedalgo stuck his thumbs between his rotund mid-section and the extra snug navy blue cummerbund, snapping it against his body. "Tight, Macho!" He snapped the cummerbund once again, giving a robust laugh. "You see, not an inch of sag."

"I'm trying," grunted Macho Muscles.

Hedalgo called toward the bus stop bench, "Mattie, my dear, did you make the arrangements for the music?"

"I did, I did," she answered, while diligently tying ribbons around small bouquets of daisies and carnations. "Wasn't it nice of Mr. Dribble, the cut flower salesman, to donate these left over flowers? They will make such nice decorations. They're hardly wilted, except this one." Mattie pitched the crushed carnation into the litter basket.

Anita the Recycler picked up a red rose from the middle of the stack of flowers. "Look, he even included a few long stemmed roses. Such generosity."

"Maybe so, but I am a good customer." Mattie held a small bouquet at arms length, admiring her neat arrangement.

A man carrying his sport coat over his arm brushed hastily by Mattie. He stopped to excuse himself. Before Mattie knew what happened, the man snatched the flowers from her grasp and slapped two quarter into her palm. Anita giggled.

"What's so funny?" Mattie asked, staring in disbelief at the two quarters.

"Not bad," Anita said between chuckles, "for someone who has tra, tra, trouble selling fresh flowers." She glanced at Mattie with a sly glint in her eyes. "And to, to, to think this corner is such a trouble spot." She raised her voice in a sing-song tease. "Those kids sure made things difficult for you."

Mattie snapped her umbrella point at Anita, who retreated with a gasp. The Recycler pulled back, her arms crossed tightly in front of her face. Anita cringed and frowned at the snapping umbrella.

Seeing the distress she had caused her good friend, Mattie pulled the umbrella back and extended her hand to Anita. "You're right, my dear, teasing or not, if I wanted to sell these wilted flowers, or even fresh ones for that matter, I'd probably be here all night. I'm sorry Anita, truly I am." Mattie gave the quarters to Anita. "Please take these to Flaggadoo. He's taking care of the funds."

"Tighter!" Macho called to his tall, slim street friend, who held the rope on the other end of the overhead sign. The man gave a yank nearly pulling Macho Muscles off the light pole, which he hung onto with all his strength. Macho grunted as he struggled to pull the rope taunt. His face reddened; bluish veins popped out on his neck, his eyes bulged. But Macho Muscles held tight, and with a last desperate jerk, he managed to tie his end of the rope in a knot. Jumping to the cement sidewalk with the grace of an acrobat, Macho landed in a squat.

Thrusting forward on his lean legs, he sprung swiftly into the air and landed on his tiptoes. He flexed his muscles in triumph.

The sign, tightly strung over Flaggadoo's Alley, was decorated with palm trees and tropical fruit, highlighted with large, bright red letters: JAMAICAN STREET JUMBLE—TONIGHT. Below it, another small sign was taped securely to a tripod made of old curtain rods. It read: DONATIONS ACCEPTED.

"Ah . . . just perfect my boy," Hedalgo sighed, stepping back to admire the decorative signs. He read each word with an air of pride, while swirling imaginary strokes in the air with a wide tipped felt marker. "I'm still not a bad sign painter, even if I must say so myself. Don't you think so, Macho?"

To show his admiration, Macho Muscles gave a pat on Hedalgo's back, who eagerly returned the gesture. A well intentioned swat it was, but a bit too much for Macho to withstand. He went flying head first into the alley, twirling his arms madly in small circles as he tried desperately to regain his balance. His legs, unfortunately, never caught up with his head. Macho landed in a throng of street people who were bustling about, preparing for the night's affair.

In the midst of the hubbub, Flaggadoo rested on an old stuffed chair. By his side stood a bewildered Ella and Stix.

"What's going on?" asked Stix, not knowing where to look first.

"Mr. Flaggadoo, please," begged Ella. "Tell us what's happening. Have all the street people gone berserk? What's all the commotion?"

Flaggadoo pushed on the chair's worn arm rests. Slowly, he raised himself to a somewhat crooked standing position. His joints cracked like popping corn. He was about to speak when Anita tugged on his sleeve. "Flaggadoo," she extended her hand. "Mattie said to put these in the Jumble Fund."

Instinctively, Flaggadoo eyed the ridged edges of one of the coins. "It's real all right. Two whole quarters and it's not even 5:45. You're not going to tell me that someone paid fifty cents to get into the Jumble. I mean, after all, I know it's been ages since we had one. But fifty cents, that's a bit much to believe."

"What's a Jumble?" asked Stix.

"Are you kidding?" Anita said directly to Flaggadoo, without so much as glancing toward Stix or Ella. "No one would pay that much. Mattie sold a small bunch of flowers to a passing business man."

"Huh!" Flaggadoo rubbed his chin and twitched his nose. "That's impossible. She hasn't sold a fresh bouquet all day, at least that's what she told everyone. And you expect me to believe she sold some of those wilted posies that old miser Dribble gave her."

"What's-a-Jumble?" Ella raised her voice.

"Yes she did," Anita assured Flaggadoo. "Some young man just bought them from her." She folded her hands under her chin and fluttered her eyes. "And he was soooooo handsome."

"A jumble," shouted Stix. "What-is-a-JUMBLE?"

"And he gave her fifty cents?" Flaggadoo jerked his head from Stix to Ella to Anita.

"Th, th, that he did, two whole quarters," Anita agreed with a nod.

"I've had it!" screamed Ella at the top of her lungs.

Followed by Stix, who hollered even louder, "And will someone please tell me, what in the world is a jumble!"

Instantly the street people ceased talking and moving. They froze like icebergs. Slowly, all eyes focused on Ella and Stix.

Quiet in the city wasn't really quiet. The dribble of water falling from the gutter into Higgin's sewer sounded much like pebbles dropping from one of the rooftops into a large puddle. Every sound of the city smashed into the alley, echoing off the battered brick walls. The hum of the restaurant fan became a roaring jet on take-off; the clicking of women's heels against the sidewalk mimicked exploding fire crackers; the argument between a passenger and a street wise taxi cab driver could have passed for the great presidential debate.

The street people waited motionless for someone to speak.

Stix and Ella dared not move. "What did I say?" Stix shrugged, his face slightly reddened with embarrassment.

Flaggadoo broke the silence, howling with uncontrollable laughter. The others joined in. Snickers, chuckles, snorts and howls echoed from every direction. Ella and Stix wanted to laugh too, but they didn't know what to laugh at.

Hedalgo stepped into their midst, his double chin shaking like gelatin. He pulled his lapels straight and tipped his top hat a tad to the right, the brim barely resting on his bushy eyebrows. "A Jumble, my dear children, is a music blast." He twisted his sleek mustache. "It's a street party, a fun fair, a rollicking festival." He spun around in quick steps, dancing a knee-knocking rock. Hedalgo raised his arms to the small strip of sky above. "A Jumble," he sang, "you want to know what a Jumble is?"

The street people answered together while pointing to Stix and Ella, who cowered behind the old stuffed chair. "They do, they do! Indeed, They do!"

"Then I will tell you," boomed Hedalgo. "A Jumble is a celebration for our street people. It will be a gas, a blast, a fun time just for you." He pointed with both hands, one index finger toward Ella and the other aimed at Stix.

"For us?" Ella said in a hush.

"That's right," Flaggadoo assured them. "And the money we make will be for your bus fare home."

Hedalgo held up his palm. "And, of course, any extra contributions shall go into the Soup Kitchen Fund."

Scattered shouts of agreement rose through the crowd of street people as they went on sweeping, decorating and preparing for the seven o'clock Jumble.

Mattie stood at the entrance of the alley, smiling brightly. Clicker was by her side. He held Skags in his arms. "I'll hang around until nine o'clock," he assured Mattie. "That way there'll be no trouble from the tough gangs on the East Side or the city officials."

Skags licked the policeman's golden badge and pawed his chest, begging for another scratch behind his ear. Mattie nudged the policeman's side lightly and whispered, "For a tough city cop you sure have a soft spot for kids."

"What do you mean?" the policeman asked.

"You know exactly what I mean," said Mattie. "This afternoon you were ready to run me and Skags in. Now, when you find out we're tryin' to help these kids, you volunteer to work overtime, with no pay."

"Look who's talking," said Clicker, setting Skags on the cobblestone alley. "You must have done a lot of quick talking to convince Hedalgo to hold a fund raising Jumble. Last time you people had one of these things, Hedalgo landed in jail for disturbing the peace. He gets carried away when it comes to supporting the Soup Kitchen."

"Crossin' my heart, Clicker. It won't happen this time. I set enough of a bad example for these kids."

Mattie watched Ella and Stix talking to Flaggadoo. "Now there's a strange relationship, Clicker. Do you know that Flaggadoo actually dated the kid's aunt at one time?"

"Who doesn't Flaggadoo know?" Clicker chuckled.

"No, seriously, he really did. And do you know that the kids spent their bus money on food for him?"

Hedalgo waved at Mattie and Clicker. He bent over and rubbed Skags behind the ear, motioning toward the kids. Skags didn't need a second prompt. He dashed across the alley, stopped to lick Flaggadoo's dangling fingers, then in one swift motion, jumped into Ella's arms. Hedalgo straightened quickly, clicked his patent leathers and snapped his lapels. "Well, my children," he said to Ella and Stix, "perhaps missing your bus wasn't so bad after all. Look at the new friends you have made." He pointed to one person after another. Each responded with a nod, except for Mattie, who slipped quietly out of the alley with Anita, Macho Muscles and Abdu Skins.

"Where are they going?" Ella asked Hedalgo.

"To fetch the music makers, dear child. We can't have a Jamaican Jumble without a Jamaican band."

"You don't think they could be the same ones we heard

playing on the street this afternoon?" Ella glanced at her brother.

Stix remembered the music makers dressed in white. "Who knows." He gave a shrug, holding his shoulders in a high taunt position. "The way things are going anything is possible in Flaggadoo's Alley."

DIMOND

CHAPTER IX

BACK TO FIGGSVILLE

At 7:00 P.M. Flaggadoo's Alley was jumping to the music of the Jamaican Jumble Band. Four men in white with open-collared shirts, the ones that Ella and Stix had seen earlier in the day, played and sang a nonstop mix of music, from calypsos to soft rock, from popular hits to the old fashioned polka. The beat was special. It was what Hedalgo ordered.

Small bouquets of cut flowers and colorful ribbons hung from fire escapes, dumpsters, ventilating fans and the variety of hooks that dangled from the dusty bricks and wooden window frames.

More than one hundred street people danced merrily on the humpy cobblestones. Some waltzed to rock music, not able to deal with the quick beat; others jumped and spun around clapping their hands and singing along with the band leader.

Anita the Recycler pushed her wheel-wiggling shopping cart past Hedalgo and Mattie. Macho Muscles slouched deep in the cart, his arms and legs dangled and swayed over the rusted wire edge. As they zoomed by, Macho reached from the cart, slapping a handful of coins upon the rickety wooden table that was set up at the entrance of Flaggadoo's Alley.

"Let's go!" he pressed Anita to move faster. "We're late."

Anita shoved her way through the street people to the center of the dancers and instantly began whirling the cart in circles, twisting her body from side to side, keeping perfect time with the music. Macho tried unsuccessfully to get out of the cart, begging his friend to stop. But Anita was too taken with the music, her eyes set upward in a dreamy state, her head bouncing as she moved.

"Dance with me, not with the cart," screamed Macho Muscles.

Anita saw his mouth moving but couldn't make out a word he said. "Oh, he just loves it," she cried, spinning the cart around and around. The street people gathered in a circle, encouraging her to continue. Anita loved the attention. She twirled her head and shook her body vigorously as she spun. Macho made one last desperate attempt to jump out of the cart. At the last note Anita came to a screeching stop, spreading her tattered skirt in a deep curtsy. Macho, who was now standing up in the cart, went sailing head over heels into the crowd. The drummer gave a timely roll, crashing the cymbals at the split second that Macho tumbled to a halt at the feet of Flaggadoo, Ella and Stix.

"Perfect landing!" Abdu cheered and applauded. The street people roared with laughter.

"Macho," declared Flaggadoo, "I see you finally made it, and what a grand entrance it was."

Anita pulled her friend to his feet. "Of course," said Macho, staggering from the spinning ride. "It just took a little longer than expected to recycle all the aluminum cans we collected this afternoon. That's why we planned this grand entrance. Some act, huh?" He gave a quick wink at the Recycler.

"Th . . . th . . . that's right," Anita agreed, hesitantly. "We were out making money for a couple of good causes. Would you believe a buck ten for the Soup Kitchen and twenty-one cents for Ella and Stix's bus fare. What do you think of that?"

The street people cheered. Mattie smiled as Hedalgo held up the JUMBLE money box. "A profitable night, I counted every last penny." He handed Mattie a handful of mixed coins. "Count this again," he said. "Should be one dollar and eighty cents to the penny, just enough for bus fare to Figgsville."

Mattie waved at the band leader, then moved through the crowd to the front of the band. The singer made a few loud clicking sounds with his teeth. "Your attention," he called. "My friend Flaggadoo wishes to make an announcement." The crowd quieted.

Flaggadoo rubbed his hands together as he often did when his knuckles ached. He looked over the street people, taking time to nod and smile as his eyes met a dozen or so people that he hadn't seen since the last Jumble. They waited for his words. He pointed to his right. "It's nice to see that the Mission Street people and the Hall of Hope group came tonight."

"Wouldn't miss it for a zillion handouts," squawked a short, toothless woman.

"Yeah, she likes her dancing too much," hollered another. "Tomorrow she'll be aching all over."

Laughter echoed through the alley. Flaggadoo smiled and nodded. "It was nice of all of you to come, whether you had a few coins to donate or not. What's important is that you're all here. The way things are going, we may be seeing more of each other at the Soup Kitchen real soon."

The crowd cheered their approval.

"At this time I'm going to ask my good friends, Mattie and Hedalgo, to come forward please."

While Hedalgo edged his way toward the band, Mattie turned to Ella. "My child . . ." she began, hesitated, then thrust the money into Hedalgo's palm and disappeared into the crowd. For a moment Hedalgo stood speechless, distressed at Mattie's behavior.

"Hedalgo, please." Flaggadoo shook his arm.

"Oh, yes, of course." Turning to Ella and Stix he said, "I'm sorry about everything that happened this afternoon." He handed Stix the coins. "There's enough here for bus fare; it's from all the special street people. Like Flaggadoo said, it's not important whether each and everyone gave money, 'cause some of us just don't have any to give, but it's how we feel about things that count. I know some of us did our share of fighting." He stretched his neck to see if Mattie was in the crowd. "And maybe it's good that we did. After all, if we wouldn't have argued, there wouldn't have been a street trial. And if we didn't have the trial, you never would have met all these wonderful people."

Skags awakened from a short snooze and howled his approval.

"That's right," said Hedalgo acknowledging his favorite little dog. "Good friends, good cause. Getting to know you gave us reason to have a Street Jumble, a reason to pull together again. Our street friends always find a way to help people in trouble. Tonight we did very well for our causes, too. In another week or two, maybe we'll have enough to pay the back rent for the Soup Kitchen, then we can start making some dough for next month's rent."

"We really miss having our Soup Kitchen open," said Anita.

"Yeah," groaned Macho, "but how are we going to come up with two hundred dollars?"

Abdu skated forward. "You mean we still don't have enough money to pay that crook of a landlord?"

"I'm afraid not," answered Hedalgo. "Two hundred bucks is a ton of money. Even if we have two more Jumbles, we will probably still fall short."

Groans flowed through the crowd.

"Two hundred bucks a month and the place is falling apart," Abdu snarled. "We ought to pitch that miserly landlord in Higgin's sewer with the rats for a few days. That would teach him what it's like to live in the streets."

Flaggadoo held up his hands. "This is no time for complaining. After all, we did raise the bus fare for the kids. Isn't that cause to celebrate."

"He's right!" shouted Anita.

Macho muscles began a chant. "Let's hear from the kids. Ella! Stix! Ella! Stix!"

The others chimed in, "Ella, Stix, Ella, Six . . ."

Flaggadoo motioned for the kids to come forward as the crowd continued to chant. Ella and Stix stood before the street people, but neither could say a word.

"What's the matter?" shouted Mattie from behind the dumpster, trying to keep a steady voice. "This afternoon you were full of words, Ella. Never heard so much gibberish come out of one mouth in all my life." Some were astounded at her remark, but Flaggadoo knew better. It didn't surprise him at all.

Ella barely managed a faint smile. *I ought to let her have it,* she thought. Deep down, she knew why Mattie was acting so gruff. It was another act, a real put-on. She kept a tight lip. Stix cowered behind Flaggadoo, fearful that Ella would start another fight.

"OK!" said Hedalgo in his commanding judge's voice. "If you won't speak, then at least you can entertain us. How about a song and dance?"

"Hooray! Dance! Come on!" came the cheers. "Sing! Be happy!"

Ella whispered in Stix's ear. He went over to the band leader and said something, then moved toward Ella. "Are you ready?" She gulped and nodded. "We have this little song and dance, sort of made it up this morning," Stix said shyly. "I'm not sure about the music, but I guess most any rock tune will do." He glanced at the band leader looking for assurance. The leader smiled and raised his hand.

"It's called Figg-A-Figg-A-Doo," sang Ella, her voice cracking a bit.

Ella and Stix started moving in a rock rhythm. The band leader nodded his head then swung his hand in time with their beat until the band started playing. Music flowed, making their movements come easy.

"Figg-A-Figg-A-Doo-Ah. Doo-Ah. Doo-Ah," sang Stix. "Figg-A-Doo-Whaaaa!"

Ella spun around several times. "Doo-Ah! Doo-Ah!" she echoed. "Figg-A-Figg-A Ooo-Ah-Ooo!"

Together they sang and danced to the music. "Figg-A-Figg-A-Doo Doo-Ah! Doo-Ah!"

The street people began snapping their fingers and clapping hands.

Ella bounced her head. "Move it Stix," she ordered. "Come on everybody, sing. Doo-Ah Doo-Ah Whaaa-O-Whaaa!"

They all answered, joining in the dancing one at a time until they were all rocking to the music, singing as with one voice. "Doo-Ah! Doo-Ah! Figg-A-Figg-A-Doo-Whaaaaa!"

Flaggadoo moved to the side of the alley with Mattie. They sat together holding hands, listening and watching the best Street Jumble ever. Flaggadoo said nothing about Mattie's rude remarks to the kids. He understood her feelings all too well.

"Flaggadoo," asked Mattie. "Is it true that you once knew the kids' aunt?"

He nodded with a grin. "She was my old girl friend, sort of a hometown sweetheart, I guess."

"Why did you ever leave Figgsville?"

"Why does anyone ever leave anywhere?" Flaggadoo answered. He rubbed his knuckles as he spoke. "You grow up, times change, feelings change, things go right, things go wrong." He patted Mattie's hand. "You know what I'm saying, don't you?"

Mattie knew exactly what her friend meant. "For us there have been some very bad times. But we will always have our hopes and dreams." She gazed at the dancing kids. "And there will always be children to think about. We must never allow them to live a life on the streets, dear Flaggadoo. You can be sure I'll see to that."

"I know what you must do," he said, his words filled with sorrow, his heart heavy with the gloomy memories of the hardships of homelessness, of lonely days and freezing nights.

They stared at each other for the longest time, feeling each other's pain, seeing past troubles, assuring each other of a hopeful future.

"Maybe things will be a little better when the Soup Kitchen reopens," Flaggadoo said softly.

Mattie turned with a jerk and snapped to her feet, pointing her umbrella right in Flaggadoo's nose, startling him a bit. "Enough of this sadness," she barked. "Tell me my man, is it true?" She snickered through her fingers. "Is it really true that your full name is Fin-i-gus Fer-din-and-o Flag-ga-doo?" Before he could answer Mattie bent over in uncontrollable laughter. "Fin-i-gus Fer-din-and-o. Oh, that's a real winner," she howled.

Clicker smiled as he paced beneath the swinging Street Jumble sign. A cool breeze eased the day's heat. He turned toward Mattie's corner. It was nearly deserted now. Only a man in a wrinkled business suit sat on the bus stop bench reading a newspaper. A bouquet of daisies poked their crumpled heads from beneath the man's pants as if they were gasping for air.

Clicker murmured under his breath, "Will tomorrow be any better for them?" He sighed deeply and moved on, keeping a watchful eye on Flaggadoo's Alley. This was his unpaid beat. The kids were his priority, but he knew Mattie and Flaggadoo would see to their safe return.

The constant jam of bumper to bumper traffic thinned to cars and buses moving swiftly by, some with their headlights glaring. The sun dipped low in the sky, full and deep orange. Skyscrapers cast shadows that bent upward at the base of buildings facing the west. Glass paneled walls reflected dancing images of distant neon signs, blinking lights and a mix of soft colors in the sky behind the silhouettes of passing jets, a portrait of dusk in the city.

The Jamaican Jumble Band banged out the last note of Figg-A-Figg-A-Doo. The department store clock chimed.

"Eight-thirty," Hedalgo announced, "it's time for the children to go. Mattie . . . Flaggadoo, will you and a few of your friends please escort Ella and Stix to the bus stop."

Skags jumped from Flaggadoo's stuffed chair. He pressed his cold nose against Ella's leg and nudged gently until she picked him up.

The band played soft Jamaican island music. The street people swayed and followed as Mattie led the children toward the end of Flaggadoo's Alley. Hedalgo tipped his hat, stood erect and waved. "Take care dear children, farewell from Flaggadoo's Alley."

Abdu Skins skated by the "greedy grate". He did a graceful short hop upon the seat of the bus stop bench, balancing perfectly on his toes. He whipped out his notebook, brushed back his slick hair and announced, "I wrote a little something. It's a poem."

Macho Muscles and Anita shifted to his side. "It's our way of saying good-bye and good luck."

Together they recited:

On Mattie's corner we came to know
Two fun filled kids who lost their dough.
At first we fought with some distaste.
When people hate, it's such a waste.
It took old Skags to make us see
We still can love and disagree.
The Jumble was a lot of fun.
So long it's been since we had one.
Raising coins for a bus ride fare,
Was cause for joy because we care.
On streets each day it's tough to live,
Easy to take . . . little to give.
Bus money you spent for dear Flaggadoo.
An act of kindness from both of you.
In just a day you won our hearts.
Good luck, Godspeed as you depart.

There was an awful hush, one that made everyone feel uneasy, a choking silence. Even the wailing of a distant siren ceased. For an instant cars disappeared from the street. The street people stood at the alley entrance still as ice sculptures.

Mattie didn't know about the poem. It made her task even more difficult.

Stix fidgeted, his eyes darting from one person to another, searching for words that were not to be had, hoping for someone to say something . . . anything.

Ella rubbed Skag's ears, who gazed upward from cradled arms and licked her chin. She nestled him close, then gently placed the little dog in Mattie's arms.

Abdu tore the page from his notebook. He crumbled it into Ella's palm. Anita shivered, touched by Abdu's gift. He never shared his writing, not even with Hedalgo.

"Do you have the bus fare handy?" Flaggadoo asked, his voice finally breaking the unbearable silence.

"Oh yes," Stix blurted, anxious just to hear his own voice. "I have it right here." He patted his pocket.

Mattie could see a bus stopped at a red light a few blocks away. Her heart ached. She knew it was time to do what she dreaded. There was no other way out. These children must never leave the streets with happy memories.

"Ella . . . Stix," she said softly, will you remember me as a wretched old witch or a tattered terror of a baglady?"

"Never!" They answered.

"But we fought like cats and dogs," she reminded them.

"We did," Ella whispered, "but things are different now. We know more about each other."

The bus pulled to the curb. Macho stepped up on the entrance platform, holding open the folding door. "Be right with you," he said to the driver.

"You may be tough on the outside," said Stix, his voice quivered a bit. "But you're nothing but a softy, no matter what you say."

Mattie grit her teeth. She had to think quickly. "What about these people? How will you remember them?"

Stix shook Abdu's hand. "I'll always remember you as a great skater and a wonderful writer. Maybe someday you will be a famous poet." He turned to Macho Muscles. "I will remember you as a hard worker, and a person that could make me laugh, even when I didn't feel like it. And Anita, you are a friend indeed, kind and gentle. And . . ." he chuckled, "the only person I ever saw dance with a shopping cart."

"You gettin' on or not?" called the driver.

"Hold on a minute," ordered Macho. "We're saying farewell to our friends."

Such a strange mix of people, the bus driver thought.

Ella reached out to pet Skags. "I'll remember this little guy. He's more than an ordinary dog. And you Mr. Flaggadoo, you are a very special person. I will tell Aunt Jenny all about you."

Flaggadoo gasped in horror. "You're going to tell Jenny about me." He groaned.

"Yes. I'll tell her all about your wonderful family. I'll tell her of your large, unusual home; about all this property that surrounds it. And most of all, I'll tell her about tonight's wonderful Jumble, er, ah, party, about the singing and dancing, the band, and all the good people who came."

Ella's eyes glazed over as she moved toward Mattie with outstretched arms. "And you Mattie, I'll always . . ."

"You'll what?" screeched Mattie, pulling back in a sudden jerk. She snapped her umbrella at Ella's feet, barely missing her toes. "Go on with you. Get off my corner!"

"But, but, but . . ."

"What's the matter little girl? You stuck for words? Take your brother and hit the road! The street people don't need the likes of you. We'll forget about ya the second you're gone."

"But, but, but . . ."

"You think the Street Jumble was a party just for you? Nothin' could be farther from the truth. It was just a way to raise money for the Soup Kitchen, and to keep ya quiet until we could get rid of ya both. You two were the best excuse we ever had to get movin' with our mission."

"But, but, but . . ."

"Hey, driver load these kids and get them out of here. Can't ya see they don't belong with street people."

The driver leaned forward. "Come on kids, you don't belong on this corner. It's getting dark." He paused while Macho Muscles moved aside. "This bus is going to Figgsville. You coming or not?"

Flaggadoo limped forward and with gentle hands guided Stix and Ella into the coach. Stix paid the driver, while Ella rushed to a seat with an open window.

Mattie was still ranting and shaking her umbrella as the bus pulled away from the curb. "Good riddance," she hollered. "Never come back either. We street people don't ever want to see you around here again. Spoiled brats!" She spat.

Tears dripped from Ella's cheeks. Stix swallowed hard. They knew Mattie was playing her tough role. "It's her way of telling us the streets are no place for us," mumbled Stix softly.

Dimond

Ella waved. "The streets are so cruel," she sniffed. "And the night is only beginning."

The bus roared away, disappearing in a cloud of black, diesel smoke. Mattie remained on the corner long after the bus departed, her shoulders slumped, her face stone-like. She waved limply, and a tear fell atop Skag's head. He flinched and licked Mattie's salty cheek.

Flaggadoo placed his arm around her shoulder. "You're a brave woman, Mattie. You did the right thing. But no matter how tough you think you were, those kids know the real truth. They know how you really feel, and will always remember you. Just like me."

Mattie forced a smile. "Anything you say dear, dear Flaggadoo . . . Fin-i-gus Fer-din-and-o Flag-ga-doo."

Together they disappeared into the darkness.

CHAPTER X

CHANGES

S tix sat by his bedroom window staring at the street
below. Things seemed different to him now. It had only
been one week since he and Ella returned from the city.

He leaned forward, inching up on his tiptoes to catch a
glimpse of the front lawn. *The grass is greener*, he thought. *And
it smells better, too, fresher, maybe.* He remembered how he wished
it wouldn't grow so fast. Mowing grass was different now. It had
a purpose. As for being boring, neither he nor Ella would talk
about that anymore.

Ella rushed upstairs and pounded on the door. "Come on,
Stix. We have a ton of stuff to do today."

Stix slipped the blue notebook from beneath his pillow.
Slapping it across his palm, he smiled and opened the door.
"I'm ready," he said, racing passed Ella toward the stairs.

Ella laughed. "Hey!" she called sharply.

Stix jerked to a stop on the fourth step. He turned his
head slowly, raising his eyes to Ella. He knew what his sister
wanted to hear. Ella leaned over the banister, tapping her

fingers impatiently on the oak rail. "Well?" she asked, a touch of sassy challenge in her voice.

"Who do you think you are talking to, Mattie?" Stix teased. Then he nodded quickly as Ella frowned. "Sorry about that." Stix backed up a few steps. He knew better than to tease his sister about Mattie. He knew how she felt about the street woman. It wasn't a joking matter. "I didn't mean that, really." He rubbed his ear as though he were punishing himself.

"Out with it," Ella demanded.

His voice softened. "I talked to Dad before he left for work this morning, just like we planned."

"Did you tell him everything?" Ella's eyes widened.

"Everything."

"Even about the street people . . . Mattie, Hedalgo . . . ah, ah?" She paused. "And Flagga . . ."

"Yeah," Stix broke in abruptly, "and I explained why we didn't tell the whole truth last week. Dad was angry at first, just like we thought he'd be, but after I explained about Flaggadoo and Aunt Jenny, he calmed down."

"He's not going to tell her, is he?"

"No."

"Oooooh." Ella sighed in relief. "I'm sure happy about that. It would be a shame for Aunt Jenny to find out the real truth about Flaggadoo." Ella sat on the top step. "I told Mom, too."

"How did she take it?" Stix was almost afraid to ask.

"Not so good. I got a lecture about the dangers of the city, and of course, about talking to strangers."

"Bet she nearly had a fit when you told her we were with street people."

"Just about." Ella bit her lower lip. "Mom said we were fortunate, but after hearing the whole story, she changed the word fortunate to down right lucky."

"She's right, you know," Stix said. "Things could have turned out real bad for us."

"Uh-huh, no doubt about it." Ella's voice waned. She thought about Mattie; about the stormy farewell; about the arguments and the street trial. *Oh Mattie,* she lamented silently,

I know what you really are, no matter what you said to us, no matter how things turned out.

Stix knew her thoughts. "Is it Mattie?" he questioned in a whisper.

Ella nodded. "She had to do what she did. Even Mom agreed, Stix. Mattie knew the streets were no place for us. That's why she acted so miserable. The crushed flowers, the street trial, her ranting and raving, everything. It was just her way of keeping us among her friends until the right time. She was protecting us, Stix."

"Do you think she knew we were lost in the city from the time we lost our quarters?" Stix asked.

"Mom thinks so, and so do I. Mattie just didn't know what to do with us. At least not until after the Jumble. Mom said Mattie must have been a very brave and caring person."

"Now I get it." Stix remembered how he felt about Mattie. "I liked her, and I didn't like her. I wanted to listen, and I didn't want to listen. I wanted to run away, and I wanted to stay." He remembered his confusion and fear. "I think you're right, Ella. What other reason would she have had to act the way she did? This makes me feel better about things. Deep inside I never wanted Mattie to be a bad person."

"Neither did I, Stix," Ella shrugged and grinned, "even though I fought with her like a cornered alley cat. Despite it all, I must admit she even made arguing interesting. Didn't she?"

"Yes. They were all interesting," added Stix. "Every last one of them."

"Sure were, but I'll never forget Mattie."

Stix edged closer to his sister. "So what are we going to do, sit around and talk about street people and Flaggadoo's Alley all day? Look Ella." He thumbed the pages of the blue book and thrust a row of neatly hand printed figures in front of her nose. "Dad said it's OK."

"So did Mom," she added. "Really liked the idea."

He sprung to his feet and tore down the steps waving the blue book in the air. "So what are we waiting for. Let's do it!"

Mr. Bowman's lawn seemed extra small. Ella trimmed faster

than Stix could mow. In no time they finished and were on their way. They crossed over Main Street and headed down the block.

"Oh no," gagged Ella. "Look what's coming."

Stix clenched his fists. "Punky Macko. Looks like we're in for trouble."

Punky walked right up to Ella, his hat tipped back as usual. "Hey Ella, what's happenin'?" He shot a high-five in front of her face waiting for a response.

Ella ducked back, thinking he was about to shove her. "Ah, er," she slapped at his hand with a weak five fingers. Then she stiffened and tightened her jaw. "Hi Punky," she responded in a tough voice, trying to hide her surprise.

"Whatcha doin'?"

"Not much," answered Stix.

"Wanna play some softball tomorrow? The South Figg gang is comin' over about three o'clock. Sure could use two more players."

Stix nearly laughed out loud at the silly look on Ella's face. He could read the shock in her eyes. "Ah, sure thing, Punky. Sounds like fun."

"You comin' too, Ella?" Punky asked.

She hesitated, then said, "I guess so, I mean, sure I'll be there."

"You're not going to cop out on me, are you?"

"Never."

"Super." He tipped his hat back until it nearly fell off and smirked just enough for Ella to notice. "We need someone that can jaw at the ump, and play second base, too. Never knew a tougher talker than you, Ella." He gave another high-five and laughed. "See you at the park tomorrow."

As soon as Punky turned the corner, they burst into laughter. "Can you believe it?" they said together, then went on their way, turning into the First National City Bank at the end of the street.

The teller glanced at the blue book. "Stix and Ella Collins's Dog Fund," she read. "Oh yes, your dad called about an hour ago. Everything is ready to go."

"According to our figures, we should have two hundred

and forty-seven dollars in our savings account." Stix pointed at the figures on the bottom of the notebook page.

"Just one minute." The teller clicked a few keys on the computer. "Make that two hundred and fifty-six dollars and nine cents. Interest, you know. But you only want a check for two hundred dollars. Right?"

"Right." Stix answered, trying to look very business like.

"I'll be right back," said the teller, and in a few minutes returned and handed Stix the check. Ella peered over his shoulder.

"Perfect," she said.

"That's the official name." Stix replied, removing a neatly folded envelope from the blue book. He attached a note to the check and slipped it inside. Handing it to Ella, he warned, "Don't lose it."

"Not a chance," Ella assured him.

They thanked the teller and started for home, taking the long way around. It was something they had to do.

At first, Railroad Avenue seemed as dead as ever. Suddenly, old Mr. Hinton sprung from his white, wicker chair, moving quickly from the porch to where Stix was standing.

"Do you hear it?" he cried, his voice filled with anticipation and excitement.

Stix felt his heart pound, thinking his chest would surely explode. Before he could say a word, two diesel engines lumbered by, the whistle blasting. One hundred and nine freight cars followed: box cars, flat cars, tankers and gondolas heaped with coal. The wheels screeched and squealed on the rusty rails. Ella held her ears and grimaced. But Stix stood with his eyes fixed on the passing freight. Only his lips moved as he counted each car silently until the blinking red light on the end of the last car faded out of sight.

Mr. Hinton smiled. "There's going to be two a day, even on Sunday. I read about it in the newspaper. This was the first one. I'm glad you were here to see it. The railroad is establishing a new route between the northern industries and the city. Yes sir," he said, looking Stix right in the eye. "It's going to be a little like old times. This town just might come alive again." He limped slowly back to his favorite white, wicker chair. "I'll be waiting every day now."

"And I will, too," answered Stix, as they moved across the tracks.

The South Figgsville Firehall was alive with music.

"Come on in and have a soda pop, said a stout fireman to Stix and Ella as they passed by. "It's the fire chief's wedding reception."

Another fireman with red suspenders danced by with his singing wife.

"That's Mrs. O'Dell," shouted Stix.

"Glad to see you're not washing clothes today," Ella called to her.

Mrs. O'Dell winked. "Not today kids," she answered, whirling to and fro. Little did she notice her screeching cat as it sped across the floor chasing a mouse, at the same time escaping the playful barks of the firehouse Dalmatian.

At the American Legion Hall, Charlie, the double chinned old friend of Flaggadoo, hollered and spun about in a frantic state. "I won, I won, I won," he chanted repeatedly. He spotted the kids and fanned out the cards, singing triumphantly, "I won, I won, I finally won."

"Do you believe it?" Stix said to Ella.

"No!" shouted the other players, who were roaring with laughter at Charlie's antics. But Charlie ignored them and continued to parade about the card table, his double chin bouncing with each proud step.

Stix and Ella talked a lot about Figgsville as they walked. "It seems that things have changed around here in the past couple of days," Ella said.

"Maybe," Stix said. "And maybe not."

"What do you mean?"

"The changes could be in us, you know."

Ella stopped and tilted her head. Stix kept on walking. He was thinking about his dreams of visiting new places and meeting exciting people. The unplanned visit to Flaggadoo's Alley was anything but a dream. It was a real adventure. Unlike the dreams, things were not all neat and orderly. There were so many things that he would never forget: torn clothes, dirty faces, soleless shoes, an alley without a roof, and above all, despite the laughing faces, he would always remember the sad eyes of the street people; eyes that lacked dreams and told of unspoken hardship; eyes that loved and eyes that hated.

Ella's voice startled him. "We're here, Stix."

"Huh! Oh yes, the mailbox."

Ella held the envelope open. "Better look it over one more time."

Stix removed the check and note. "Two hundred dollars exactly," he said.

Ella glanced at the note. She read, "For the Soup Kitchen." She remembered how long it had taken them to write so few words. All the other letters they had written, there must have been at least a dozen of them, didn't seem quite right.

"Short and to the point I'd say."

Stix nodded in agreement.

She refolded it, attached the note, and sealed it in the envelope and dropped it into the mailbox. She sighed. "There goes our dog. But you know something brother, I feel real good about what we just did."

"And so do I," echoed Stix.

They walked the last block in silence, completely unaware of the shaggy, black and white stray mutt, who pranced softly at there heels.

LaVergne, TN USA
05 May 2010
181685LV00002B/4/A